EVERY STEP HE TAKES

THE BRIDES OF PURPLE HEART RANCH BOOK 8

SHANAE JOHNSON

THOSE JOHNSON GIRLS

CHAPTER ONE

"Left. Left, right, left."

The sounds of boots marching on the ground should've been thunderous, imposing. In reality, it was more like the sound of grade school children let out of the back of the school for recess. That was likely because none of the boys and girls assembled had reached their majority. They were also marching on fertile, green farmland and not pavement.

"Billy, I said right, not left," shouted Private Mark Ortega. "Do you know your right from your left, son?"

"Yes, sir," said the scrawny kid who was no thicker than a bean pole. "It's the one we say the Pledge of Allegiance with."

Mark resisted the urge to pinch the bridge of his nose when Billy started to raise his left hand, then yanked it down in favor of his right one. Mark couldn't help a glance at his watch. Not because he was ready for the hopeless training to end. He wanted more time to teach these cadets the drill. He knew that for most of them, the Army was not just a way out, it was the only way up.

"All right," said Mark. "Let's try it again."

There were less than a dozen kids gathered. They ranged in racial identity from porcelain skinned Jordan Scott to the tall cup of coffee that was Ayden Benson. The kids also ranged in socioeconomic backgrounds to the polished black oxfords worn by Janey Marsden to the worn sneakers of Billy Trent.

"Left," called Mark. "Left, right, left."

Once again, Billy lifted first his right foot and then his left foot. He collided into Janey, who then bumped into the brick wall that was Eli Wilson.

Janey halted. With clenched fists, she turned to glare at Billy in a way that made Mark wince. The young woman was going to make a fine Army soldier.

Billy, on the other hand, might make a great Marine. That bunch didn't need to know their left from their right out in the water swimming with the fishes.

"At ease, everyone," said Mark. "At ease."

The small group of seventeen and eighteen-year-olds relaxed their stances at Mark's command. For the past year, the Purple Heart Ranch had invited the town's youth to the land for enrichment programs. Aside from the original mission as a rehabilitation ranch for Wounded Warriors, the ranch had developed a specialty of working with troubled adolescents and teens. Which made sense since many of the soldiers there had come from a troubled past.

Mark's past wasn't troubled. He'd come from a loving, close-knit family. Though his family ties had been strong, life still hadn't been easy.

He'd come to the ranch broken after the dregs of combat. With a medical discharge, he'd found healing of his own after only a couple of months on the ranch. Mark hadn't wanted his military career to be over, but it would appear that it was God's will. With his time left on the ranch, he was determined to dole out as much of himself as he could to the next generation of service men and women.

"I'm sorry," Billy mumbled to Janey and Eli. "Sorry, sir," he said to Mark, not quite meeting Mark's gaze.

It was another thing Mark wanted to work on with the kids; building confidence. The soldiers manning the ranch put the kids through their paces taking care of the farm animals, learning to work with and ride horses, and tend to the lands. Those programs had flourished, making a positive impact on each kid that came on the ranch and turning more than one life around for the better.

In the last two months, they'd added a new program; a Junior ROTC program. Mark's hand had shot up as a volunteer to work with the kids. He enjoyed nothing better than rising each morning and taking the would-be soldiers through their paces. Unfortunately, their pacing was part of the problem. His troops were constantly out of step with one another.

"The last drill of the day is to hit the pivot."

Mark saw a number of the kids wince. Marching wasn't as easy as it looked on television or in the movies. The kids struggled with staying in their simple formation and keeping their spacing. He knew pivoting, turning a corner, would be a challenge for them. But as he'd learned when he was in his high school's JROTC at their age, if you never pushed yourself, you'd never go anywhere.

And so, Mark gave the command. First to march. And then to pivot.

Just as he predicted, the pivot didn't go as planned. Billy turned left instead of right. Only this time he bumped into the wall of Eli. Down Billy went, nearly getting trampled by Janey who had perfect form, spacing, and pivot. Mark knew he had to get in there before Janey made the boy road kill. But before he could bark an order, he saw something else out of order. The sole of Billy's shoe was hanging on by a thread, or rather what looked like dried glue.

"All right, that's enough for the day," said Mark. "You all know what you need to work on for next time."

"Sir, yes, sir," the kids bellowed, nearly in unison. If unison sounded like an echo off a large cliff where the sound bounced around a few times before dying off.

Mark reached out his arm to Billy. The boy took it. Mark hefted the young man up, but Billy's gaze stayed cast down.

"I'm sorry, sir," said the boy. "I'll work on it some more tonight. I'll get it the next time, I promise."

"I have no doubt," said Mark. "It took me quite a while to get the hang of all this."

"It did?" Billy's gaze lifted, hope shining in his eyes.

Mark gave the kid a nod. "You headed back to the barn to get your stuff?"

"Yes, sir."

"Mind if I walk with you?"

"Yeah, that would be cool. I mean, yes, sir."

"It's fine," grinned Mark. "At ease."

The two took off. Billy had to march double time to keep up with Mark's casual gait as they walked the path from the pastures to the barn designated for the youth program. In the distance, Mark saw amputees mounted on thoroughbreds. Each man and woman wore content smiles on their faces. Mark understood why. He'd come from combat with all his limbs and most of his mental faculties, but he knew the power of commanding such a majestic animal restored something in a soldier's spirit.

"I'm glad you were able to keep coming," Mark said to his young charge. "I know you had a conflict, having to watch your younger brother."

"It got sorted," said Billy. "He's in the after-school program at the church. Pastor Patel set it up."

Mark knew that. The pastor had arranged for the fees to be paid so the younger kid could attend the program his wife ran. The Patels had done it quietly as Billy's mother had a reputation for being proud and not accepting handouts.

"I had to do that a lot when I was your age," said Mark. "Take care of my younger brother. The kid was a pain, but he was my pain."

Billy nodded but didn't offer any elaborations on his situation. Honestly, Mark hadn't expected him to. He had been the same way in his youth.

"You doing good in school?" Mark tried another way past the kid's defenses.

Billy shrugged. "I don't get the best grades, but I'm not failing."

This kid could've been living Mark's past life. Mark hadn't been a scholar by any stretch. His grades were normally just barely above passing. He'd only put in the effort because he didn't want to disappoint his parents. Plus, he had to graduate. His family didn't need another high school drop out with no job prospects to take care of. Money had been tight since before he was born, and the situation had never loosened up for a single day after.

They were the last to arrive at the barn. Most of the kids were already on the bus to take them back into town. Billy's well-used backpack sat on a patch of dirt just inside the door.

"Hey," said Mark, "you live near the consignment shop, right?"

Billy nodded uncertainly as he pulled the dingy straps over his shoulders.

"Would you mind dropping these shoes off for me?" Mark grabbed a shoe box off one of the tables inside the barn. "They were a size too small. I got them thirty days ago, so I can't take them back."

Mark took the pristine sneakers from their box. He had to maneuver quickly to hide the sales tag that still hung from the laces. Mark wasn't sure if Billy noticed as he placed the unblemished soles in the palms of the kid's hands.

"Actually," Mark continued, "they look like they might fit you. You want them?"

The accommodating smile fell from Billy's face. His skinny elbows had been bending as he brought the shoes to his person. With Mark's last words, he straightened his elbows and handed them back.

"No, thank you," said the kid.

Mark didn't take the shoes back. "You'd be doing me a favor."

"I know what you're trying to do." Billy placed the shoes back in the box on the table.

Mark sighed. Yup, this was his teenaged self to a T. Taking donations and gifts from strangers had always left him feeling dirty and inferior. As though he were a stain on society that someone with money had to wipe out. He preferred going through hardship than to confront that feeling.

But this was different. Mark wasn't a stranger to this kid. And this wasn't a handout. The kid needed the shoes to reach his dream. He certainly couldn't keep marching when his sole was damaged.

"Look, kid, it's not a handout. It's a leg up. I want you to succeed. We need men like you in the service. But you're not going to get ahead if you can't take a step in the right direction."

Billy pursed his lips. Mark could see he was wearing him down. He decided to try another tactic.

"You'd take them if we were family, wouldn't you?"

Billy hesitated. His features screwed as though he knew there was a trick on the horizon.

"It's what soldiers do for each other. When you're a unit, you're family. I'm the head of your unit, which means I'm pretty much your father. So, do as I said and take the shoes."

Huh. Look at that. It worked.

Under that command, the resistance went out of the kid's shoulders. Billy sighed, letting go of all his tension and pride. He took the shoes.

"Thank you," he said, once again not quite meeting Mark's gaze.

That was fine. Mark had some time to work on that. But it wasn't much time.

"Now, go home and practice that march."

"Yes, sir."

Mark watched the kid hurry to the bus. He felt a strong sense of pride well in his chest at what he'd done. When he shoved his hands in his pockets, they were empty. Those shoes had cost him a pretty penny that he hadn't had to spare. But that's what family did for one another, and the people on the ranch were all family.

Unfortunately, his time on the ranch was almost

up. He knew he could come and visit the people there whenever he wished. Mark just wished he could be the one to keep leading these kids into the bright future they all were trying to get to.

CHAPTER TWO

The room was an explosion of white. Alabaster white walls boxed the ladies inside. Ivory white curtains hid them from outsiders' views. Cream colored carpeting ran under their heeled feet. A porcelain chandelier hung from the ceiling illuminating the lace, chiffon, and tulle that exploded from every corner.

Honey Dumasse smoothed the fabric of her pearl-white gown. The material was exquisite to the touch. She tried to keep herself from touching it over and over again for fear she'd leave a stain. But her hands were as pristine and clean as always. Every strand of her hair was in place, even though she'd been in and out of gowns all morning.

There had been the A-line ivory gown that flared

from her hips. Honey hadn't had the bust line to support the gown. Then she'd tried on the eggshell-colored mermaid dress. Only her figure was more of a flat board and not the curvy hourglass that the dress shape demanded. Then she'd stepped into the pearl-colored drop down gown.

The strapless gown put the focus on her shoulders instead of her bust line. Her honey-blonde hair was lifted up to accentuate the dress's lines. The skirt had a flare, but that flare started at the calves and not her boyish hips. It was perfect.

All three gowns had been specially made for her. Each one had a price tag that was the down payment of a house, and there were no returns. Her father had told the seamstress to spare no expense, not that he ever looked at the price tag of anything.

It was appearances Sugar Daddy was most interested in. And he wanted his little girl looking picture perfect for her big day so that everyone could see. She was his only daughter to come out in the debutante ball, so he'd needed her to make a big impact.

"Where's your sister, Honey? Shouldn't she be helping you?" asked Mrs. Klein. The older woman had had three daughters come out already, each to a glowing success that had declared one after the next Klein sister the Belle of the Ball.

Honey plastered on a bland smile as she lifted

her gaze in the mirror. Her smiles were always bland, never big and bright, never too small or pinched. Bland was just right. No one could say she was trying too hard or too little with this smile. They couldn't say she was trying at all.

"Ginger is out of town today."

"Oh, you mean she's off on the campaign trail?" Mrs. Klein wrinkled her nose in distaste.

The thought of working women always brought on such derision in this cluster. Yes, it was the twenty-first century. But they were society women. With the money in their bank accounts, there was no need to lift a finger outside of charitable work. Especially if you were as wealthy as the Dumasse family.

"I think what Ginger is doing for the community is admirable," Honey spoke up for her sister. Not because she believed in her sister's cause. It was because she knew that weakness was a liability.

Ginger insisted she was doing the highest form of charity work by serving her community. It was not a notion that the ladies of the society, or their father, shared. Henry Dumasse took his eldest daughter's political career as an affront to his wealth and position of power. If Ginger needed to work, then his company, Sugar Daddy's, would be seen as lacking.

Just another reason everything needed to be perfect for Honey's coming out in the debutante ball.

Starting with the dress. Looking at the reflection again, she realized it was only *almost* perfect. Something was missing. She just didn't know what.

A mother would know. But her mother wasn't in the picture. Her father had erased her from their lives, quite literally. He'd even had her painted out of the commissioned family portrait.

"I think I know what that dress needs, my dear," said a kind voice.

Honey's gaze shifted in the reflective glass. She slipped, and a real smile broke through her bland expression as Mrs. Patel came into view.

"What do you think about these shoes?" asked Mrs. Patel.

"Yes," Honey breathed. "They would be perfect."

Mrs. Patel handed the beaded, white heels to Honey. She slipped them on and saw that they did indeed complete the outfit. In fact, she decided they had to make their debut at the Bachelor's Brunch tomorrow.

"It just needs one more thing." Mrs. Patel reached behind her back and unclasped a necklace resting there. It was a simple chain with a heart-shaped pearl at the center. When Mrs. Patel approached her, Honey shook her head.

"Oh, no, Mrs. Patel. I couldn't—"

"Nonsense," the elder woman said as she clasped the necklace around Honey's neck. "You should always have a family heirloom for these things. And you've been such a help to me raising money for the Sunday school program, it's the least I can do."

It was a stretch of the truth. Honey hadn't been that much help to the Sunday school effort. At least not with her presence. But she had worked her contacts and helped to raise a majority of the funds that would support the effort for another five years.

She'd had to do it quietly as her father didn't believe in supporting church efforts. Henry Dumasse had yet to find a way to bribe God, so he didn't give His house much attention. That meant the family didn't give the church much attention.

But Honey had fond memories of going to Sunday school while her mother did Sunday Bible study. Even though she hadn't been to church in years, much less Bible study, Honey always tried to find a way to help the church that had once brought her so much joy.

"That dress is a good choice on you," said Mrs. Dumbarton. "It gives the illusion that you have something in the way of hips. You want the gentlemen to see that so they know you can carry plenty of babies."

Honey inhaled and exhaled through the tight bland smile. "Thank you for the advice, Mrs. Dumbarton."

The funny thing was, the woman was truly

trying to be helpful. The end goal of all this fuss was another piece of jewelry; a few carats worth of an engagement ring.

Most modern-day debutante balls were no longer about the marriage mart. In New York City, many of the women coming out were already successes in their own right. In the big cities, the balls were more of a networking opportunity to meet and greet the movers and shakers of upper-class society.

But that was New York. This was Montana. And the truth was, Honey was husband shopping.

Jackie Onassis had been a debutant, and she'd married a Kennedy. True, John cheated on her, a lot. But it had happened after they were married, and she'd been locked into the security of the union.

Unmarried women had it hard back then and today. Divorced women had it harder. Honey had no intention of becoming one of those kinds of women.

She had her sights set on Beau Bryant, the most eligible bachelor in the whole state. His family was wealthy, so Beau wouldn't be after Honey's trust fund. He would be handed his own business once he finished college. And when he did, he would need a high society wife to be on his arm at events, to run his household, and to stand beside him in this society. Honey had been trained for just that job.

In fact, she'd been trained for only that job. At

twenty-one, she had bypassed college in favor of spending time at high society dinner parties and charity events. It cost about the same, but she was far better educated to handle the role in life she'd chosen.

She was ready to leave the uncertainty of her home and find some job security. All she needed to do now was get Beau to escort her to the debutante ball. Then her future would be secure. She had the dress, she had the accessories, she just needed to ask the man.

It was the only non-traditional thing about the entire process. Tomorrow, there would be a Bachelor's Brunch. After mingling and getting a feel for each other, the women would take the initiative to ask out the men.

Honey had no plans to mingle. She'd walk in wearing the outfit she'd planned, zero in on her quarry, and monopolize all of his time. The competition was small but fierce. She truly only had a few girls to worry about.

Hayley Tyler was having an affair with the gardener, so she wasn't truly interested in marriage. Sienna Bell had her sights set on college and a career. Honey's only true competition was Quinn Ford.

"Honey, don't you look a picture," said Quinn as

she sashayed in an off-white mermaid gown that accentuated her paid for bumps.

"Me? Don't be silly," said Honey. "You're going to outshine everyone in that gown."

Bland smile met bland smile. And it was on.

"I hear you still don't have a date to the ball," said Quinn.

"Well, no. Not yet. I'd like a chance to meet all the bachelors at the brunch." Honey knew better than to tell her frenemy the name of the bachelor she was most interested in. "At the brunch, I plan to see who would be most interesting and who I have the most in common with. It would be dull to spend the night of the ball talking with someone who had nothing in common with me."

"That's a very good plan," said Quinn. "Well, I'm headed off to brunch with Mrs. Bryant. She wants to introduce me to her son. Have you met him? His name is Beau. Our fathers go way back."

Honey clenched her teeth. Her bland smile dipped. But she grabbed hold and yanked it up before Quinn could see that she'd gotten under her skin.

"I think I'll try your tactic and see if Beau and I have anything in common," Quinn was saying. "If we do, you'll see us together at the brunch this weekend. Tah."

Honey pressed her hands to her dress, uncaring

of whether she got a stain on the fabric. All was fair in balls and bachelor hunting. She just had to hope that Beau was smart enough to see through Quinn's facade on his own. But come tomorrow's brunch, the pearls were coming off, and it would be all-out war.

CHAPTER THREE

Mark brought the horse down from a gallop and back into the corral. He hadn't grown up riding the magnificent creatures having been born and raised in an inner city. But over the past two months, he'd taken to riding like he'd been born to it. Too bad he'd only have a couple more weeks to ride whenever he pleased.

"You're looking good up there, soldier."

Mark turned to grin at Dr. Patel. The man was one of the pastors of the town's church, but he was also the psychologist on the ranch. Mark had often wondered if the two professions contradicted each other. But Dr. Patel brought a certain spirituality to how he healed ailments of the mind.

He'd certainly helped Mark his first few weeks there. Now Mark was managing his PTSD symptoms. Too bad Dr. Patel wasn't a financial planner because that's where Mark really needed the help.

"I was just here for the ride," said Mark, as he brushed the horse down. "I let her take me where she wanted to go."

Dr. Patel laughed. "Keep that attitude with human women, and you will be successful in your love relationships."

Mark had no desire to be in a love relationship at the moment. Even if he had been looking for someone, he couldn't possibly take care of them financially. He would never have a wife and family without being able to take care of all their needs. He was, for all intents and purposes, unemployed and not easily employable.

With only a high school diploma and an honorable medical discharge from the military, there wasn't much he had to offer. What little he did have, he funneled right back to his family, trying to keep their heads above the rank waters of poverty.

"I'm gonna miss this place," said Mark, as he finished putting the horse back in its stall.

"You won't be going far," said Dr. Patel. "As I understand it, you and the sergeant are opening a recruitment center in town."

That was the plan. But they were having trouble securing a location. It was always something with the zoning in this town. Be it the zoning of the location they were looking for the recruitment center or zoning restrictions of the ranch that said all inhabitants had to be married if they planned to live on the land permanently.

Like all unmarried, enlisted soldiers and veterans, Mark and Chase had only been allowed to stay on the Purple Heart Ranch for three months to convalesce. As neither man had any intention of following the tradition of the soldiers who'd come before them and marry a woman for the keys to one of these houses, they would be out on their rears in less than a month's time.

Mark looked off into the distance where the cabin he'd been staying at rested. It was the nicest place he'd ever stayed in in his life. It housed two bedrooms, which he had all to himself. Even though he often found himself sleeping on the couch as he'd done back at home in his parents' two-bedroom apartment that they shared with his two other siblings.

"I wouldn't worry," said Dr. Patel. "Miracles happen every day in this place."

"We're working on the location," said a familiar voice.

Sergeant Colin Chase marched over to them. The man had a march that the JROTC cadets would envy. The sergeant moved with his shoulders back, head high, and long, evenly spaced strides. His walk was much like a certain terminator he'd been nicknamed after.

"See," grinned Dr. Patel.

"In fact," Chase said when he reached them, "I just found a possible building for us to put the recruitment center in. It's owned by the Sugar Daddy company and a man named Henry Dumasse."

Dr. Patel wrinkled his nose. It was a rare occasion to see the man show distaste. Mark had assumed the doctor's optimism knew no bounds. But a line seemed to have been drawn around the name of Dumasse.

Mark chuckled to himself. If someone placed a strong emphasis on the wrong part of Mr. Dumasse's name it would come out sounding highly inappropriate. Mark caught the smirk on Chase's face. Apparently, the ever-present middle schooler was alive and well in both men.

"You know him?" asked Mark.

"Not well," said the psychologist. "I knew his wife a long time ago. She and her daughters would attend church. But Mr. Dumasse never did."

Dr. Patel looked off into the horizon. He often did that in sessions when he was deep in thought. Mark had also caught him gazing off during his church sermons. After the pregnant pauses, he would say something profound that touched Mark and the rest of the parishioners deeply.

When Dr. Patel turned back to them, he simply shrugged his shoulders. It wasn't the reaction Mark expected. Not for a man of the cloth who believed every soul could be saved.

"His daughter, Ginger, still attends church," Patel continued. "She's a great asset to the community. And his younger daughter is very involved in charitable work. She helped fund the Sunday school program my wife runs."

"Maybe we can talk to them," said Chase. "Let them know what a great thing this center will be for the youth in the community."

"Dumasse is a hard man to get in to see," said Patel. "But I know where he will be. He'll be at a brunch tomorrow."

Mark frowned at the term. He'd never understood the purpose of brunch. Why take two meals and smoosh them into one? Especially if you weren't poor? Brunch was a rich man's meal.

"My wife happens to have some tickets to the event if you two would like to attend."

"That sounds great," said Chase volunteering the two of them.

Mark held back. The ever watchful sergeant had missed something in Patel's gaze. Mark had seen that look in the doctor's eye before. Right before Brandon

Lucas met his wife Reegan Cartwright. And then again before Reece Cartwright proposed to Elsbeth Barrett. Patel had a hand in most of the marriages arranged on the ranch. It was a touch Chase and Mark had studiously avoided their time there.

"You'll have to wear your uniforms," Patel was saying.

"Not a problem," said Chase.

Mark stood quietly. He crossed his arms over his chest and waited for the other shoe to drop. Or rather, for the cupid's bow to let loose its arrow. He bounced on his toes in preparation to duck.

"You might get picked up by rich women," Patel grinned.

Now Chase was catching up. His eager grin turned upside down. "What exactly is this brunch?"

"It's called a Bachelor's Brunch. It happens before a debutante ball. It's where the young ladies who are about to come out into society go to find an escort for the ball."

Mark took two steps back. He'd already shut down when the good doctor had said they would be high society women. That was another phrase for stuck up, rich girls. Mark did not mix with that breed unless they were out slumming. He'd done that once and gotten burned for it when the woman pretended she didn't know him the next day.

He knew why she'd shunned him after their

rendezvous. He wasn't from money, and the copper smell of the pennies he pinched clung to him like cheap cologne. But Chase held his ground. He turned to Mark with a look of determination.

"We gotta go," said Chase.

"You're welcome to go," said Mark, taking yet another step back. "But not me."

"We're in this together. I need you to have my back. Especially with those dimples."

Mark swatted Chase's hand away from his face.

"We don't even have to talk to any women," said Chase. "We can just go in and meet with Dumasse, tell him what a great thing the recruitment center will be, and ask for him to consider leasing the building to us."

"What if a woman asks us to be their escort to the ball?"

Chase raised an eyebrow.

Mark pursed his lips.

Then the two men burst out laughing.

"Yeah, right," said Mark. "Like they'd choose one of us."

"I don't see the joke," said Patel. "The two of you are good, strong, courageous men. Any woman would be blessed to have you as an escort."

That's why Mark liked the man. Dr. Patel was a believer when it came to love. Especially when he was trying to direct one of his patients to heal their wounds with the elusive emotion.

Mark's unit had come to the ranch as a four-man fire team. Brandon and Reece were both happily married, and those marriages had truly healed their wounds. But the ranch had already rehabbed both Chase and Mark without brides. They now had a different mission.

Unfortunately, it looked like their path would meander into a day of bumping elbows with the rich folks to accomplish their mission. Fine, he'd suck it up. Besides, there was no way a man like him would get chosen to escort one of the high society ladies anywhere.

It appeared like a castle in the sky. Only there were no turrets. The Dumasse Estate was one of the first mansions built in the state of Montana. Honey's family's money was old, nearly as old as the state itself.

The Dumasses had started out as farmers but not humble ones. They'd bought up most of the fertile land in this and neighboring towns. Once they had a monopoly, her forefathers then leased the land to the farmers who made their way west. Later, during times of tumult and depression, the Dumasses bought back that land and raised the rents.

Landowning was only a small part of their fortune. Sugar beets were the family's bread and butter, or rather, bread and honey. The turnip looking plant was used to make granulated sugar, brown sugar, powdered sugar, and more.

That elixir was packaged up and sold as part of the Dumasse Sugar Daddy company. Sugar was a mainstay of modern life. It was in everything, which meant that walking out of a grocery store each shopper would be taking home a bit of Dumasse into their cupboards. Her father's reach was everywhere.

Honey's driver pulled the luxury car up to the gates of the sprawling property. Once upon a time, this land had been crops. But her grandfather had not preferred the working men and women of society be so close to his humble abode. So, the land had been turned and was now miles of private, manicured pastures.

It took a few minutes to drive the long road through those pastures to the massive plantation style mansion at the epicenter. Once at the massive front steps, the driver came and handed Honey out. He went to take her bags, but Honey stayed him. It was only four bags this shopping trip. She could manage.

She was eager to get inside to her room and decide which dress would go best with the shoes she'd picked out for the Bachelor's Brunch tomorrow. The one she had purchased yesterday would no longer do now that she knew Quinn was on the warpath. So, after her fitting for her ball gown, she'd made a couple of stops to find the perfect cocktail dress to fit her plans.

Honey did allow the driver to open the front door for her. It was a massive oak, likely one hundred years old. Even with her hands-free, she often had a hard time getting into the door of her home. The door made a creaking sound as the hinges gave way. The squeak died out beneath the raised voices coming from the hall.

Both Honey and the driver halted on the threshold. The driver, being a good servant, averted his gaze and affected a dispassionate smile as he bowed and closed the door behind them. Honey, being a dutiful daughter, plastered on her bland, unaffected smile as her father's booming voice shook the plaster.

"Do you have any idea what your little antics are doing to my reputation?" Henry Dumasse bellowed.

"Do you have any idea that my career has nothing to do with your reputation?"

Honey recognized the even-toned voice. Her sister had had the same upbringing as Honey. They both knew that women were not to raise their voices or show too much emotion, especially in the face of men. Most definitely not in the face of their father.

Like Honey, her older sister, Ginger, had been

sent to finishing schools. There they learned manners and deportment. But only Honey had actually finished school. Ginger had always had a different vision for her life.

"I'm not asking you for any of your money," Ginger said, exasperation slipping through her inflection. "I'm not even asking for your vote."

"Good. Because I'm voting for your opponent," said their father. "Women have no place in politics. They don't have a head for business."

Honey stayed frozen in the foyer. Whenever people argued, she had a habit of staying as still as a bug in hopes that they wouldn't see her. Just like when her mother and father used to argue. Only, her mother never actually opened her mouth to defend herself. She'd just take whatever her husband had dished out to her in poised silence.

"You forget that I was at the top of my class in high school and college," Ginger countered her father's assertion.

"Useless degrees." Honey could imagine her father's meaty hand slicing through the air at the ridiculous notion. "Not worth the money I paid for them."

"You didn't pay for college, I earned a scholarship."

Ginger's words were clipped. Her voice had also raised an octave. Honey could hear them both breathing hard. Still, she held her place, clutching her bags tightly in her fists.

Though she would never run. Not like her sister had. Not like her mother had.

"I don't know why I even came here," said Ginger. "Maybe out of some delusional hope that you would support me, not with your money, but with ..."

Ginger let the sentence drift off into the abyss that had struck up between the two of them. Her older sister had reached her majority, so she didn't need her father's money. Her trust fund was now in her possession. Every once in a while, Ginger would return home to try and bridge the distance with her father. Henry Dumasse would always take another step back from his eldest child.

Honey knew her father had a good heart. He'd kept a roof over her head. He'd made sure she'd had the finest clothes. He'd made sure she ran in the most elite circles. Wasn't that how parents showed love? By providing.

Their father had provided for his two girls even through his disappointment of wanting boys to carry on the family name and business. He'd never let them forget that they'd failed him from the start at their births. That's why Honey was determined to be a success and marry the son he never had. Well, one of the reasons why.

"If a woman disagrees with you," Ginger was saying, "you cut her off. Just like you did with Mom."

"Watch your tongue." Her father's voice dipped dangerously low.

The air changed on the entire ground floor. It felt like a heat wave passing through a hot desert. It was safest when Henry Dumasse raised his voice. When he lowered it, it was time to take cover.

Ginger knew better than to challenge their father with that tone. "I'll show myself out."

Honey heard her sister's footsteps coming near. She didn't want to be in the middle of this argument. She always made it her business to stay out of any argument that involved the man who provided for her. Unfortunately, despite the heat of the argument, her legs hadn't unthawed from their frozen mode.

Ginger appeared in the hallway. She looked more like her mother than Honey. Despite her name, Ginger was a brunette, like their mom. But all three of them had the same crystal blue eyes.

Ginger's face softened when she saw Honey. "Hey, honey bunny."

"Good afternoon, Ginger."

Ginger's smile fell by a degree. She didn't mention the formality of her baby sister's greeting. Her gaze went to the bag's clutched in Honey's hands. "Shopping?"

Honey dipped her head. "For the Bachelor's Brunch."

Her sister's smile went down another degree. Honey knew Ginger detested the Debutante Ball and all its trappings. She had walked away from her come out ball in favor of campaigning to become the youngest state politician in the region at twenty-one.

"Whatever you wear, you're going to look beautiful, honey bunny."

Ginger came to her, arms open wide. Honey stiffened. If her sister noticed, Ginger ignored Honey's tense state. Ginger wrapped her arms around her as though they were little girls again.

Honey couldn't help it. Her bottom lip trembled, losing its grip on her bland smile. She shut her eyes for a brief moment and allowed herself to relax in her sister's hold.

A creak of a floorboard brought Honey's eyes open. Her father loomed in the doorway. Henry Dumasse narrowed his bushy, blond brows at the two. Under his glare, Honey wiggled in Ginger's hold.

"Goodbye, Ginger."

Ginger's smile was completely gone when she released Honey. She ran a hand down the side of Honey's face. "See ya, honey bunny."

The front door opened and closed with a quiet

snick. When Honey looked up, her father was gone from the doorway. She was left alone in the quiet foyer. She was often left alone in this house. Soon, she was the one that would be leaving, she promised herself as she headed on quiet feet to her room.

CHAPTER FIVE

Mark had never considered himself to be socially awkward. He was always the life of the party. He'd just never been to a party where one wrong move could cost him his entire bank account, plus a few pints of blood. And maybe his right arm.

He'd never been inside a place so fine as the Chateau du Planturex. The carpet looked like it had been shaved off the backs of tiny chinchillas, sewn together using golden thread. The curtains were fine lace but such a high thread count that he couldn't see through the fabric. Intricate glass vases sat in every corner with long, lush, colorful flowers that looked out of this world.

Mark kept his arms at his sides in fear of making one wrong move. He moved in a straight line to ensure he didn't put a foot out of place and bump into something he couldn't ever hope to repay.

And then there was the food.

He'd never been to a brunch a day in his life. If he missed breakfast, he simply ate lunch. He didn't know what to do with this combination of the two meals.

There were mini dishes that looked like egg omelets, but were far too colorful and filled with vegetables that should not accompany a yoke. There were tiny pastries with intricate sugary decorations that all had a 3D effect. And he wasn't sure, but he thought he saw snails on one of the silver platters. The things that looked like tiny blueberries, he'd learned were fish eggs. With his stomach turned, he decided to skip eating and focus on the reason they'd come there so they could leave as soon as the task was complete.

"I'm glad we're not splitting the check," Mark said to Chase.

The sergeant looked more at home in the high-end setting. But Chase stood rigid, far more stiff and stoic than his normal stance in the military. Clearly, he wasn't comfortable being back in his former life.

"Don't worry, buddy, I would pay," he said. "You're a cheap date. You'd just order a bison burger."

The mere thought of one of Montana's bison

burgers or elk burgers brought Mark's stomach back to life. He couldn't wait to get out of this she-she poo-poo place and get some real food. Along with a slice of huckleberry pie instead of the little girl's tea party dishes that were available here.

The two soldiers were inside a grand ballroom with overhead chandeliers. Everyone was dressed to the nines. Many of the men wore uniforms. Mark had learned many of them were from military schools. But there was an equal number of men in tailored suits and ties. Those men, he'd learned, were from Ivy League schools.

Mark kept his distance from both. He had nothing in common with the suits. And he couldn't stand the green noses in uniform who had yet to know a day of combat and might never.

The women were another story. They were like porcelain. Pretty to look at, but he didn't dare touch one of the delicate creatures. He'd had his hands in the mud that morning. There was still dirt in his nail beds.

He gave his cuffs a tug. The fabric fought back. His watch had caught on the lining. The timepiece was an heirloom passed from his grandfather to his father to Mark. It was old and crinkled, and it didn't keep perfect time. But he wore it because it reminded him of who he was and where he'd come from.

"There's our guy," said Chase, his back stiffening even more. "Henry Dumasse, the CEO of Sugar Daddy."

Mark looked over at the guy. He was a big bruiser of a man. He looked like a wrestler that had been stuffed into an expensive suit. But the suit, it suited him. Definitely custom made.

Henry Dumasse reminded Mark of a drill sergeant. He watched as the man cut the weaker men in his path with glares until they parted the floor for him. He silenced others with a downward turn of his lips until they sank down into seats. This was the man that stood between them and their recruitment center?

"Mr. Dumasse." Chase stepped directly in the man's path, back straight, gaze unflinching.

Mark fell in step at his back.

Mr. Dumasse peered down at Chase. Though both Mark and Chase were over six foot, the older man easily had a few inches on them in height as well as width.

"Sergeant Collin Chase." Chase stuck out his hand, aiming it for the man's middle. "I believe you know my father, Stuart Collins of Sunstone Banking and Financial."

Dumasse's glare didn't lose its hard edge. But there was a twinkle of recognition in his eyes. He took Chase's hand and engulfed it with his own.

Mark could've sworn he saw Chase wince at the man's grip.

"This is my colleague, Private Mark Ortega."

Mark reached out his hand, preparing for a crushing shake of his own. But Dumasse didn't offer his hand. Instead, he wrinkled his nose, the flint returning to his gaze. He left Mark's hand hanging there.

Mark's empty hand curled at his middle. His feet shuffled until he was back behind Chase. Mark had no officer's title or rich family name to recommend him. Why was he there again?

"I did some business with your father," Dumasse was saying to Chase. "I don't recall meeting you during any of our interactions."

"I decided to go into service for my country," said Chase.

"Seems a man's first loyalty is to his family. But I assume you'll be taking over for your old man when you're done playing toy soldier?"

Mark had served under Chase for over a year. They had been dropped into some harsh conditions during those times. Mark had never seen the man flinch. At Dumasse's last statement, a slight tick began at the corner of Chase's right eye.

"No, sir," Chase said stiffly. "I think I can do more good serving my country on the home front than behind a mahogany desk."

Now Chase got the flint sneer. "Good?" said Dumasse. "What good?"

"My colleague and I are opening a recruitment center," said Chase. "It will be an opportunity to talk with the youth of the town about the benefits of enlistment and a career in the armed forces. It would give them a purpose."

"Let me guess, you're looking for a donation?"

"Not a donation." Chase shook his head. "A lease. It seems you own the property we're interested in letting. I'd love to make some time with you to-"

"Bryant," called Dumasse with a sharp toothsome grin. "Been waiting for you to arrive."

Dumasse walked past Chase, bumping him in the shoulder and putting an end to the conversation. He shook the hand of another gray-haired man. Beside the newcomer stood yet another young man in military dress. The rank on his pristine uniform marked him as a second lieutenant, the highest rank that could be achieved for a student in a military academy.

"That went well," said Mark.

"I know men like him," said Chase. "That was just the intro meeting. We need to show him we won't back down, gain his respect."

"So, we can go now?"

"Not yet. Let's not waste this opportunity. There are other movers and shakers in this room."

"Well, you go move into the crowd. I'm gonna go shake a leg outside for a minute and then head out."

They had brought separate cars as Chase had come from the location in town and Mark from the ranch. Mark clapped Chase on his back and then made his way to the doors that led out back. The moment he stepped outside into the warm breeze, he felt all the constraints of the last half hour he'd spent inside the chateau loosen. He took his first deep breath and stretched his arms without fear of collateral damage.

The sound of a frantic feminine voice brought his attention around. The voice spoke quietly, quickly as though asking questions and also answering them.

Peering around a sculpted bush, the deep breath Mark had just inhaled stuck in his throat. Standing on the other side of the rose bush was the most beautiful girl he'd ever seen in his life.

Blonde hair like sunshine. Blue eyes like the waters of a clean pool. She wore pink, the same shade as the roses. But her beauty made the flowers look dull. And she was indeed talking to herself.

It looked like she was giving herself a pep talk. Mark couldn't hear her words, but her actions spoke volumes. She opened and clenched her fists for emphasis. She nodded her head as though that would force the truth of the words down into her soul.

Finally, she took a deep, cleansing breath. Then she took a step forward, only to catch her heel in the cracks of the pavement. Her forward momentum halted. She very nearly toppled to the ground. Luckily for her, Mark rushed into action.

CHAPTER SIX

Everything was perfect. The designer dress she'd had custom made highlighted all of Honey's best assets. Her hair was done up to sleek perfection framing her heart-shaped face. Her professional makeup job shimmered in the afternoon light. And the shoes were the knockout portion of the ensemble.

The golden straps crossed her petite ankles. The slim stem of the shoe lifted her arch and did wonders for her calves. She felt like Cinderella. If Cinderella had her father's credit cards and not a fairy godmother.

Also, unlike fairy magic, Honey's ensemble wouldn't vanish at midnight. These would stay in her closet after this momentous day. Not that she would ever wear the outfit again. Dumasses never did repeat showings.

With her chin up, her bust line high, and her feet strapped in, she prepared to go and meet her future. Her father would be waiting inside to introduce her to Beau Bryant. She'd learned that Beau had just gotten into town the other night. So, there was no way that Quinn Ford had had a chance to interact with him.

Honey still had the advantage. She turned on her heel. Her body lurched forward, but her foot didn't move. Her shoe had been caught in the cobblestones.

She tried to raise her foot. But the golden straps trapped her ankles inside the shoes. She'd have to bend down to undo the strap. Unfortunately, the boning of the dress made that difficult, and she almost toppled over. She immediately straightened.

She tried wiggling her foot but was so afraid that the stem would break. She was even more afraid that the smudges of dirt from the cracks would smear her stem. What was she going to do?

Even now, Quinn was probably inside talking Beau's ear off. They were probably even talking about her. Quinn would certainly drop Honey's name casually. With an innocent smile and guileless gaze, she'd match innuendos and allusions to Honey's name, meticulously picking apart her character with nothing but friendly chatter.

Honey is as lovely as a bee, always buzzing around in everyone's ear. Implying anything that he might tell her wasn't safe. Which wasn't true. Honey was not a gossip.

Have you ever been stung by a bee? Wait until you meet Honey. Implying that Honey was vindictive. But no, that was Quinn. The woman never met a grudge she didn't hold on to.

Honey knew the game. Everything was fair in love and husband hunting. She might have done the same. Only anything she might've said disparaging about Quinn would've been true.

"Can I give you a hand, ma'am?"

The voice sent a delicious buzzing sensation down her spine. The tone was deep and resonant. It washed over Honey's back like warm syrup. She turned to see where such a voice had come from. She let out a tiny gasp when she saw that the face did the voice justice.

Twin dimples stared back at her. They arrested her before his eyes did. Dark, coffee colored eyes that she could've gotten lost in. But it wasn't time to get lost. She had to get free.

She saw that the man was an officer with his uniform covering his very broad shoulders. He was a big man, but he wasn't as broad as her father. Her father's size was imposing. This soldier's size looked warm and welcoming, perfect for hugging.

But hugging wasn't what she needed right now. She needed to get her shoe loose and get into the banquet to snag herself an appropriate escort for the ball and for life.

"Yes, sir," she said. "If you please."

The soldier walked toward her. Honey had the impulse to step back. That is if she could've. Not out of fear. With every step this man took, she felt something big coming her way, something that would change her life forever.

"What seems to be the problem?"

"My shoe appears to be stuck."

"It's like you're Cinderella," he said. His grin was a bright planet with two twin stars on the polar opposites.

"Yes, but instead of fleeing the ball, I'm trying to make an entrance into brunch."

He wrinkled his nose at the word *brunch*. That was curious. What person didn't like brunch? It was breakfast and lunch foods all at the same time, the best of two worlds.

"Right," he said, rubbing his hands together. "Let's see what we can do. Two heads together will certainly win against a shoe."

He reached out toward her leg. His fingers nearly grazed her ankle before he jerked his hands back.

"I'm so sorry," he said. "May I?"

It was not at all proper, having a stranger put his hands anywhere on her body off the dance floor under the watchful gazes of plenty of chaperones. But Honey had no choice. She had to get free.

At least that's what she told herself as she gazed down at his strong, capable hands hovering around her bare ankles. She could've asked him to go get help from another woman. But, for some reason, she didn't want him to leave.

Honey nodded her head, giving him the permission he sought. With another three-point smile, the officer ducked his head and took hold of her ankle. Honey sucked in a breath at the first contact.

His fingers were warm and gentle on her skin. They set off trickles of sensations that ran the length of her legs. Her heart skipped a beat at the points of impressions that he made.

"Just loosen the strap, and I can step out," she said.

He cradled her ankle with his left hand. Though most of his palm cupped the back of the shoe, she felt a sense of security, of being sheltered by him. It was an unfamiliar feeling in her life with a volatile parental figure. The soldier's thumb fumbled and fiddled with the clasp.

"I'm afraid I'm not all too good at taking off a woman's shoe."

Honey wondered what he was good at taking off a woman?

She gave her head, and those errant thoughts, a shake. Looking down, she saw that her dress still covered most of her leg. He was having some difficulty managing her dress, keeping her modesty intact, and wrangling the shoe.

Her head shot up as someone walked past the door. If someone saw them in this position, it would not be good for her reputation. Especially if it got back to Beau. Or worse, Quinn.

"Get up, get up, get up," she urged the soldier.

The soldier shot up, but instead of moving away from her, he pulled her to him. This position would be even worse. So, why wasn't she pulling away from him?

His chest pressed into hers. Her hands fluttered down to rest on his biceps. She thought he might try and kiss her, but his head was turned away from her.

He wasn't trying to seduce her. He was trying to protect her. Of course, he was. He was a soldier.

"What is it?" he demanded. "What's wrong?"

"I ..."

He looked down at her. Coffee colored eyes bright and alert. Her heart pounded so hard, as though she'd had a triple espresso shot ... three times. She was sure he could feel her heart beating against his chest.

"Someone was walking by," she said. "If we're caught together, it wouldn't be good."

"Oh." He blinked. The strong, dark roast of his gaze dulled. "Right. We wouldn't want that."

He let her go. She wobbled in place. His dimples were no longer out, and his lips were drawn into a thin line. She felt she'd hurt him and that knowledge hurt her.

"They're gone now," she said.

He nodded. He hadn't looked behind him. He had taken his gaze off her. It was trained on the ground, and he worried his bottom lip. She wasn't sure why, but her strong rescuer looked vulnerable.

"I'm sorry," she said.

His gaze lifted to hers, eyes searching. She had no idea what he was looking for. But something deep inside her was rising to the surface, eager to give it to him.

"Would you mind?" She pointed back to the ground, down at the predicament she was still trapped in.

The soldier sank back to his haunches. With deft and sure fingers, he tugged the strap loose and freed her.

Honey stepped out of her shoe. She felt exposed with him being so close to her bare foot.

"All better?" he asked.

"Yes. Thank you."

He wiggled the shoe. "It looks like you got it good and wedged in here." He wrapped both hands around the shoe and was ready to pull when she stopped him.

"Don't hurt the shoe."

"Don't hurt the contraption that had you trapped?" The soldier let out a low chuckle. The dimples were back as he looked up at her.

"They're hand made." Honey gave a helpless shrug. She knew men didn't understand women's obsession with shoes. But she also knew that when the right shoe was present, they couldn't take their eyes off a woman's leg.

"So, we'll just leave it there?" he asked.

"I don't know?" She looked down at the shoe that completed her outfit. She couldn't go into the brunch without it. "This is a disaster."

Honey took a step. When her bare toe met with warm concrete, she hopped. He caught her in his arms before she could topple.

The feel of being in this man's arms felt right. She'd been right about the size of him being perfect for hugging. She was only in his loose embrace, and it was better than the hugs her mom used to give. But this was not the man she was supposed to be with. She took a step away from him, but something tugged her back.

"Sorry, it's my watch," he said. "It's got a chink in the band."

The fissure in his timepiece had caught in the side of her dress. First her shoe. Now her dress. Could this day get any worse?

"Hold still," he said.

But she was already tugging away. It was at the same time that he was trying to tug in the opposite direction. The sound of expensive, custom made fabric ripping was the sound of all her hopes and dreams turning back into pumpkin seeds at the stroke of midnight. The delicate fabric tore at her hip, exposing her thigh with a peek at her backside.

His eyes went wide, as did hers. They both stood frozen in place. But there was no way they could turn back time. This was a reality, and it wasn't done.

"Honey, are you out here?" Her father's voice boomed, overtaking the light afternoon breeze.

The soldier grabbed him to her again. He gathered the ruined fabric and put her back to his front. But it was already too late.

Henry Dumasse rounded the corner. The older man blocked out the sun. But even in the shadows he cast, it was clear something was afoot in the garden.

"What's going on here?" her father demanded.

Honey might've been able to explain this away to her father. She might've been able to sneak off and climb into the town car that had brought her here, get home, change into another dress, and arrive a little more than fashionably late to the brunch and still keep up appearances. Unfortunately, her father wasn't alone.

Honey's future flashed before her eyes as she saw another man in uniform walk up beside her father. Beau Bryant came to stand at attention next to her dad. But that wasn't the worst of it.

Coming up behind Beau was Quinn Ford. There was triumph in her nemesis' gaze. There would be no need for innuendo or allusions when the reality was too good to be true. Honey was ruined.

CHAPTER SEVEN

It went beyond getting her dress dirty with his unkempt hands. He'd now divested her of her shoe and ruined the fabric of the dress. Mark's hands continued to fumble as he tried to hold the material to her body while also shielding her from prying eyes. The only way he could win this particular battle was to turn her around, her back to his front, and keep her exposed body from the gathered crowd

But things went from bad to worse when he looked up at the onlookers to see the Sugar Daddy, Henry Dumasse, gaping at them. The older man's mouth moved like a fish out of water. His lips flopped around, gasping in the open air as though the air were choking him. His eyes were big, bugging out of his head as though he were straining like a cartoon character. His huge meat-grinder hands balled and curled into fists, also opening with the tips curled as though he wanted to reach out and dig his nails into Mark's neck.

Mark knew the situation looked bad. It looked as though he'd assaulted this poor, young woman. Not that she was poor. He'd seen the bottom of her shoe. It was blood red. He'd caught enough *Sex in the City* episodes to know what a red bottom shoe meant. It meant money. She was from money, and he had his lower-class hands all over her.

This could be explained. Surely, she'd tell the man he'd meant her no harm, that he was, in fact, helping her out of a jam. Luckily, things couldn't get any worse.

"Daddy?" his damsel said.

Now, Mark was the fish out of water. But instead of bugging out of his head, his eyes felt as though they had sunk down into his sockets. His lips puckered as though he tasted the salty brine of seaweed. This could not be happening.

"Take your hands off my daughter," growled Mr. Dumasse.

Mark obliged. His hands went up in the air, as though he were under arrest. Unfortunately, they hadn't completed the job of unsnapping his watch. So, the moment he put his hands up was the same moment that more fabric tore.

Mark immediately pulled her back to him, using his arms to cover her modesty. She was trembling now. Her small form shaking like a leaf in a storm in his hold. Mark's instinct was to pull her closer. But each time he touched her, it turned into an even bigger disaster.

"I was helping," Mark began. "Her shoe was caught. And I lifted her dress to-"

Not the best choice of words.

"I wasn't trying to undress her," he corrected. "I was only after her foot."

And there went another wrong turn.

"I don't mean I have a foot fetish or anything like that. I don't even like feet."

Why was he still talking? When he opened his mouth, he made it worse. When he moved his hands, he made it worse. The best course of action was probably to keep perfectly still.

By now, a crowd was gathering. There was the young officer Dumasse had ditched them for earlier. The man lifted a brow at Mark, looking between him and the girl. The young man's jaw tensed, revealing an aristocratic cleft in his chin.

Mark felt the woman in his arms stiffen under the young officer's perusal. In response to her discomfort, Mark pulled her even closer to him to get her out of the line of inquisitive eyes. For the first time in their encounter, she struggled in his hold.

"It's true what he said." Her voice trembled when she spoke. Defeat colored her soft-spoken words, as though she didn't believe anyone gathered would see the truth. "My shoe got stuck, and he was trying to help and ..."

Her words trailed off at the sound of someone giggling. No, that wasn't giggling. It was snickering. A better word would be cackling.

The girl standing behind the toy soldier threw her head back as though she were a witch and just needed her broom. She turned on her heel without the flying device. Once inside the doors, she stopped the first person she saw, another girl in an expensive dress. The cackler pointed at the woman in Mark's arms. Then she stopped another, and then another.

Mark felt the body of the woman in his arms deflating like she was a balloon whose ends had just been untied. He was certain that if he didn't hold onto her, she would float away on the soft breeze. He wrapped his arms even more tightly around her. Though she didn't seem to notice him anymore, she did sink into his hold.

Henry Dumasse's gaze was locked on the young women behind the glass pointing and jeering at his daughter. Then he turned to the young man in uniform. The toy soldier at least had the decency to avert his gaze. Finally, Dumasse turned to face his child. The glare etched into his features made Mark, a man who had faced down the Taliban, want to take a step back for his own protection.

"If you want to go off cavorting in gardens," said Dumasse, "then you're no daughter of mine. You're just like your mother."

Mark felt her sharp inhale of breath. She had been so deflated a moment ago that when her shoulders went back and they struck him right in the chest. Again, his hold tightened. He wanted her to know that she had his support.

For his part, Mark couldn't understand what he was hearing. He couldn't understand what he was seeing. Why wasn't her father coming to him and taking his daughter from his arms, putting her care and comfort into his own arms where it belonged. Instead, he left the matter to a stranger.

"I disown you," Dumasse said to his daughter. Then he turned to face Mark. "And you, you want to toy with what's mine to try and force my hand?"

"No," said Mark. "That is not what happened here. I didn't even know that she—"

"You won't get that property," said Dumasse. "I won't have trash like you turning the good young men in this town into scoundrels."

Mark wanted to correct the man, to let him know that the military was open to both men and women. But he felt now was not the time. Especially not since Dumasse was marching out of the garden and around the path.

When Mark turned back, the crowd had grown larger. People pointed and snickered from behind the glass door. The toy soldier was making his way through them, not looking back at the scene he'd walked up upon.

The woman in his arms collapsed into him. A protective instinct came over him, and he swept her off her feet. She weighed next to nothing.

Mark cradled her in his arms so that she wasn't exposed to the leering crowd behind the glass. She turned her face into his chest. As he carried her away, the wetness he felt soaking into his uniform nearly broke him.

CHAPTER EIGHT

*D*ark blue was the color of devastation.

That was all Honey could see as the tears leaked out of her eyes. She wasn't a crier. She had been given too much in life to feel sorry for herself. Her father had given her the finest foods, the most coveted wardrobe, and a sprawling shelter. But he never failed to remind her that they were all his belongings that he gifted to her. Because all those items were gifts and not her earnings, he could always take them away.

"It's all right," soothed a deep voice. "I've got you."

She wasn't hearing the baritone notes with her ears. She felt them vibrate across her forehead and touch her eyelids. The words bypassed her ears entirely and sank into her heart.

"It's not the end of the world."

Blue was the color of deception. It was a cool balm against the tear that had ripped her life in half. One moment, she was on top of the world, at the cusp of her destiny. The next, her entire future was slashed from her hand like tattered lace.

"He'll cool down in a bit."

Blue was the color of desolation. Without her father's protection, without the hand of a man and his ring, she was alone and unequipped for the world. She had no place to go. No one to turn to.

Even now, she could still hear the echoes of the snickers and whispers of her peers. Upper-class society was not a community of caring individuals. It was a dog eat dog world, and Honey had just been stripped of her pedigree.

"You can stay right here with me until he comes for you."

Honey blinked her eyes once, twice, until the blue of her soldier's uniform came into stark focus. Seeing it clearly now, it looked far more black than blue. Looking up to meet his gaze, she saw that the center of his eyes was more hazel than coffee, as though there was a splash of cream to stave off any bitterness.

She knew there was no bitterness in this man. His insides were likely more sweet cream. He smelled sweet, earthy with a hint of something, well, sweet. Honey couldn't help but stare for a long moment as she drank him in.

He brushed a tendril of hair behind her ear, and she shuddered. It was more touch, more tenderness than she'd felt in years. And like a caffeine addict, she instantly wanted more.

"Your father was upset," the soldier said. "He couldn't have possibly meant what he said."

Yes, he could. Yes, he did. He'd meant every word and would enact everything he'd said.

Her father had divorced her mother, cut her off, and made her life unbearable for defying him. Even now, he barely tolerated his eldest daughter for choosing to live with her mother instead of him in the custody battle. He'd never forgiven Ginger for that embarrassing act, and he never would.

And now Honey had caused a scene in front of people he felt should be impressed by him. Henry Dumasse did not countenance embarrassment, whether accidental or not. He meant what he said when he'd disowned her.

Honey was ruined.

"I'll talk to him later," her soldier was saying. "I'll let him know it was all my fault. I'll let everyone know it was all my fault."

He was trying to come to her rescue again. She didn't want to tell him she was already doomed. What she wanted was to stay there on his lap while he stroked her back, crooned comforting delusions, and brushed her hair from her face.

But she couldn't. It was still entirely improper. She didn't even know his name.

"What's your name?"

"Ortega. Private Mark Ortega."

"Pleasure to meet you. I'm Honey. Honey Dumasse."

"Pleasure to meet you, too. In light of the circumstances."

The light of the circumstances? There was no light. Things were dark. Private Ortega clearly wasn't from this world. He didn't know how it operated.

It was the twenty-first century, but a girl's reputation was worth its weight in gold in her circles. Literally. Now that she was found with a stain on her person, thanks to the rip in her dress, she no longer held a place at the big table. Luckily, her soldier's lap was comfortable.

"I'm afraid you're mistaken about my father, Private Ortega."

"Please, call me Mark. I feel we know each other intimately now."

Heat rose to her cheeks. Honey stood, wobbly as she was still in only one heel. Then she clutched at the ruined fabric to cover herself.

"I'm sorry," he said, standing as well. "That was

crass of me. I have a tendency to joke when things are serious."

"Things are serious. I've been humiliated in front of all of society. I've been disowned. I have nowhere to go."

Now that she was out of Mark's lap, the panic was starting to set in. Her fingers flew to her chest as her heart began to pound. She turned away from him, in the direction her father went. Then turned back when she realized she was still indecently exposed. She became breathless with indecision and lightheadedness threatened.

"Okay. Okay." Mark held up his hands like a tamer approaching a wild lioness. "I'm sure you're exaggerating."

Honey flashed her eyes at him like a cat at night.

"My bad." He stepped back, hands now raised in self-defense. "Did I mention that when things are serious, I say things that would make a woman cut me?"

"Duly noted."

Mark lowered his hands. "I just mean, your father couldn't really mean what he just said. Family doesn't cut each other off. They're, well, family."

"Not my family. Either you're perfect, and you abide by Sugar Daddy's rules, or you're out. I've embarrassed my father and made a spectacle, which makes me no longer perfect."

"I think you're perfect." His deep voice was soft, just barely above a whisper, as though he hadn't meant to say the words out loud. He turned away, his features contorted in a sheepish grimace.

Honey stood in a ruined dress, with one shoe on, black streaks streaming down her face, and her hair disheveled. He couldn't be serious. Yet he looked at her as though she were nectar, and he was a bee.

"Oh, Honey, my dear girl. There you are."

Honey looked up to find Mrs. Patel coming toward her with open arms. Honey let go of her dress and allowed the woman to enclose her in an embrace. She didn't feel the same safety as she'd felt inside of Mark's arms, but the hug was soothing nonetheless.

"Are you all right, my dear?" Mrs. Patel ran a hand down her face and then brought her into a second hug.

Belatedly, Honey realized that her backside was exposed to Mark. Before she could reach for the ruined fabric to shield herself, she felt cloth being draped around her shoulders.

Private Ortega had taken off his blue jacket and draped it around her shoulders. She was drowned in the coat and drowned in his dark roast smell. The weight of the coat and the masculine smell lessened her anxiety like a weighted blanket used for dogs during a thunderstorm.

"Mrs. Patel," said Mark. "I'm glad you're here. Can you sit with Ms. Dumasse while I go and find her father? I can let him know this is all my fault and his daughter is blameless."

Mrs. Patel squeezed Honey's shoulder. She participated in this world, but she was not immersed in it. She knew the score.

"I don't think that would be wise," said Mrs. Patel. "I'm afraid Mr. Dumasse is an impulsive man. He doesn't cool off quickly."

"So, he's just going to turn his child out in the meantime?" Mark's brows were raised in a mix of incredulity and disgust. Disgust won out and colored his handsome features. "What kind of man would do such a thing?"

Honey knew she should defend her father and his character, but she was too caught up in someone defending her. Besides, Mrs. Patel had the right of it. What she'd described was exactly the man that her father was.

"We will figure this out my darling," said Mrs. Patel. "We can call your sister."

"No," said Honey, a bit more vehemently than she'd intended. "She's on the road for her campaign."

"All right then. In the meantime, you'll stay with my family."

"I couldn't," said Honey. "It's nearing the

holidays, and you'll have your entire family over. There won't be any space for me."

Truthfully, the Patels were her only option. She couldn't go running to Ginger, not when the two sisters had made such different decisions for their lives after their parents' divorce. Honey knew no one else in high society would offer her shelter.

"You could stay with me."

Both women turned to look at Mark.

"I have a spare bedroom at my cabin on the ranch," he continued. "This is all my fault. The least I can do is give you shelter until your father sees reason."

CHAPTER NINE

Mark's pick-up truck crunched and sputtered over the paved gravel of the drive on his way up to the Dumasse estate. He hadn't seen Chase on his way out. The superior officer had already ducked out of the brunch by the time Mark had handed Honey into the loaner vehicle he sometimes used on the ranch.

He didn't have a car of his own. He'd never had his own vehicle. His entire family had shared the same clunker since he was in elementary school. The pickup truck was a step up as it had two working doors. But the seats were still a bit crummy.

Mark had done his best to wipe them down before he'd lifted Honey inside. They'd saved her shoe, though the heel had a few scuff marks from its cobblestone captivity. He'd laid down some napkins he'd scavenged from the glove box. The richest girl he'd ever known was now sitting on a McDonald's cushioned passenger seat.

The drive to her home was long and silent. Mark had turned on the radio. But when Tim McGraw's *My Little Girl* came across the wires, he turned the radio off. They sat in a comfortable silence for miles.

And then more miles after he entered the curlicue gates of the Dumasse estate. It felt like they were on the driveway for an hour. In reality, it was probably more like five minutes. But who had a driveway that took five minutes to maneuver?

Mark had known Honey was rich before he'd known her name. She'd reeked of wealth. Literally. She smelled like a fine, delicate fragrance that was not present in nature; floral and sugar-coated with notes of sunshine.

He marveled at the lush, yet empty land they took to get to where she'd rested her head every night. Surely, she was a treasure that needed to be guarded. Maybe those guards were hiding in the rows of manicured shrubbery. But no one jumped out and halted Mark or his clunking vehicle.

And then the house loomed down on them. The mansion, or was it a castle, rose up into the skyline, making Mark feel even smaller and less than worthy. No one came out of the house as he pressed his foot, and the brakes squealed at the end of the driveway.

"You live here?" Mark asked.

"Not anymore," she said.

"But you did. How big is your family?"

"It was just me and my dad."

"Just the two of you in that big house?"

"Well, there are servants."

"I'm sure they outnumber you. It would seem it was their house."

Honey shrugged. Her gaze was on the steps that lead to the massive door. Her hand was on the door handle of the truck. But she made no move to get out.

Mark had only known this woman for an hour or so, but he knew she wasn't doing well. It was all a shock. He couldn't imagine his family disowning him, and for something so trivial. At least she wasn't crying any longer.

"It's probably best if you stay here," she said when he came around to hand her out of the truck.

"Afraid I'll break something else?"

"You couldn't make it any worse," she said as she stepped down. When she looked up into his face, her eyes went wide with sorrow. "I'm sorry, I didn't mean it that way."

"You don't have to explain. I'm clearly not from this world. I don't get all the rules." Her words had stung a bit. What soothed him was the fact that she hadn't let go of his hand. "I don't care what you say, no man could disown his child for something like this. Let's just give him the night to blow off steam. He'll call you in the morning."

The lift of her perfectly plucked eyebrow told him that she didn't believe his words. Mark still couldn't imagine it to be true. She was the man's little girl. All girls deserved protection.

Mark walked her up the steps, but he didn't accompany her into the house. Truth be told, he was scared to march inside that heavy door. He'd been out of his depth at the brunch. The majesty of this place was alien to him. Though he felt guilty for letting her go in there alone.

Forty minutes later, she emerged in a sundress and carrying a shoulder bag. But behind her were three servants carting luggage. Expensive-looking brown luggage with the gold crowns of a particular French designer. It was the large kind that would rack up charges on a commercial flight.

"I packed light," she said as she climbed back into the passenger seat.

Mark only nodded.

The servants gave him cool gazes as he closed the bed of the truck with the pricey luggage laying on hay. Mark climbed back into the driver's seat. It took three tries to restart the engine. When they were on their way, the truck moved slower under the weight of the luggage now in the back.

"You doing okay?" he ventured.

"I'm still numb. It hasn't sunk in. I guess I kinda figured this day would always come. I was walking on eggshells all my life around him, knowing anything could set him off."

"That's no way to live."

"That's why I wanted to find an escort at the Bachelor's Brunch. Escorts have been known to turn into husbands."

"So, you want to get married to get out from under your father's thumb?"

"It's the only way for a girl like me."

"The only way for a girl like you?" he parroted.

"I was raised in high society. I know, in some places, girls have many accomplishments and go to Ivy League schools. But in my family, if women aimed to achieve a career, it reflected badly on the male providers. It meant the men were lacking in some way."

That made no sense to Mark. His mother had worked every day of her life, rarely taking any day except Sundays off to go to church. And then, sometimes, she snuck in a shift after service.

"While other girls went to college, I was expected to attend dinner parties and organize charity events and talk with my father's guests. It was my on-the-job training, I suppose. And I'm good at it. I've been preparing for marriage my whole life."

Mark had learned about women's rights and women's liberation in the textbooks of school. But he'd lived the need for it in his everyday life. Every cent his mother and sister brought into the household counted, and it needed to count as much as each man's. In the Army, his life often depended on the training of the woman at his side. Equality wasn't a notion in his world, it was a necessity.

"Was there a particular bachelor you had your sights set on?" In the second after he asked the question, his stomach turned. The idea of Honey with some other man made his teeth clench. He gripped the wheel, squeezing the leather covering until a thread came loose.

"Yes," she said, her gaze fixed out the window. "He was there. He was standing next to my father when ..."

The toy soldier? Mark hadn't had any interaction with the man, but he knew the type. He was all training and no experience. A man like that wasn't equipped to take care of a woman like Honey.

But he was? Mark was the one who had ruined everything she'd worked for with a careless tug of his wrist.

"Now, he'll never have me."

"Good," Mark growled.

Honey turned to him. She tugged her bottom lip

into her mouth. Her hands smoothed down the soft fabric of her intact dress.

"What I mean is, he's not good enough for you," said Mark.

"You don't even know him. You don't even know me."

"Oh, I know enough. Guys like him are not husband material."

"And guys like you are?"

"Yes. Eventually."

Honey tilted her head to the side and regarded him. Mark squirmed under her assessment, certain he wouldn't pass muster for a woman like her.

"Guys like me are good family men. We take care of our own, even if we struggle to do it our whole lives. Guys like me work hard for what we get. Guys like him are given it."

"That's the kind of girl I am. I was given everything. I've never had to work a day in my life. And like I said, I don't know how to."

Her hand went to her stomach. Her shoulder caved forward. She fidgeted in the worn seat as though she couldn't find a comfortable position.

"And here I am depending on another man," she continued. "A stranger at that. If you weren't around to take me in, I don't know what I'd do."

"You don't have anyone else? What about your mother?"

Her features darkened. "My mother passed away."

"I'm sorry."

She offered him a bland smile. He saw through it. He saw the pain she was trying to hide from him.

"Mrs. Patel mentioned your sister. Do you want to call her?

"I ..." Honey didn't finish the sentence.

What kind of family was this? A father who could turn his back on his daughter. A sister who she hesitated to call when in need.

"This world you come from," he said, "it seems backward and not high at all. I would never turn my back on someone in need. And I'm as low class as they come."

"You're not low class." She sat forward, her gaze as fierce as her words. "You're an honorable man."

"Honor doesn't pay the bills. Your father isn't going to give us the land to open a recruitment center. That will ruin my career and my ability to earn money for myself and send home to my family."

Honey was quiet again. He left her to it, obviously having said and done enough for one day. But a few miles later, she turned to him. There was a spark of brightness in her blue eyes.

"I have a crazy idea," she said. "Maybe we can help each other."

CHAPTER TEN

"So, let me get this straight," Mark said as he cut the wheel for a hard right turn.

Honey gripped the seatbelt strap as Mark maneuvered through the winding roads of the Montana countryside. She'd never been in a car that had gone above the speed limit. None of her drivers would've dreamed of pressing the gas pedal so hard.

She had her driver's license because her father had bought her a Rolls Royce for her sweet sixteen. But she'd only driven it the once; on her sixteenth birthday for pictures and for the crowd of high-class society gathered celebrating with her.

That crowd had been mostly her father's associates and colleagues. It was all for show. Just as much of her life had been while left in her father's care. She'd played her part since her mother had left. She'd been the shiny trophy that he'd adorned and dressed to display his wealth. She'd gotten behind the wheel that day. All the while, she'd been so anxious that she might crash into something or, worse, someone.

She'd driven at the exact speed limit that day. It was what was expected. She'd smiled and waved for the photo ops. Mark drove like no one was watching, especially not police officers, intent on pulling over speeding drivers.

"You think you can find another location for the recruitment center," Mark continued, "and convince the owner to lease it to us?"

"Yes." Her response was strangled as he took another hairpin turn twenty miles over the posted limit.

"But the only way to do that is for us to pretend to be dating?"

"Yes."

The green of the trees blurred. Her life wasn't flashing before her eyes. She hadn't done enough with it for that. It was just a blur.

A blur of images of her smiling blandly while doing her father's bidding. Trying to be perfect and shiny and bright to please him. She knew he wouldn't be pleased with her new plan.

Honey couldn't believe she'd suggested that she and Mark take on the farce; to pretend they were a couple to restore her good standing and gain interest in his cause. But desperate times and all. If there was one thing she'd learned from her father, it was that she had to keep up appearances at all costs. Since she had no money, she had nothing to lose.

"By now everyone thinks that something happened between us," she said.

"I helped you out of a jam." Mark threw up his hands.

Honey gripped the edges of her seat. Another turn was on the horizon. With just the thumb of one hand, he took the turn with ease. She'd have been impressed if it wasn't her life in his hands. Or rather, his thumb.

"They won't see it that way," she said after filling her lungs with much-needed air. The windows of the pickup truck were cracked open since the AC wasn't in working order. "Even though it's true. It's more entertaining to think we did … something else."

"And now you think we should do something else to make it real?" Mark's brows rose so high they reached his hairline. The truck slowed to normal speed.

"No!" Honey's cheeks heated. She let go of the seat and folded her hands primly in her lap. "I mean, we should pretend."

She took a deep breath and began again.

"We need to make them think we're together, that we're in love. That's a better story than you debauching me."

"Debauching? What is this, the eighteenth century? Honestly, if anyone did the debauching, it was you to me."

The breeze from the cracked window slapped her in the face. She had to blink a few times before she could turn around and face him. When she did, his dimples were deep with glee.

"Can you please be serious?" She turned to face forward, head held high. The breeze now slid past the smoothness of her forehead. "You said your livelihood was on the line. If this works, you get that back."

"And you?"

"I get welcomed back into the society I was born into."

"But you'll have to do with a low-class guy on your arm in the meantime."

The crease returned to her forehead. She turned to him again. He had an aristocratic nose, a chiseled chin. There was nothing low class about this man. She wanted to tell him that but she had no idea what was in his wallet or where his family line began.

"Why don't you approach the toy soldier?" said Mark. "It's him you want."

Honey thought about Quinn going after Beau,

the man Honey had set her sights on. Honey didn't *want* Beau. She *needed* him to survive. By all accounts, he was a good man. By his account ledgers, he was well off. They would be perfect for each other. She could've been the sparkle on his arm, the shining centerpiece at his dinner parties. It was what she was meant to do in life.

"Beau and I hadn't been formally introduced yet. And then, when he saw me, my skirts were up. It wasn't my best look."

Mark scrubbed a hand over his face. Honey didn't like the remorse in his coffee dark gaze. His eyes were meant to be vibrant with life. She didn't want Mark to regret coming to her rescue. It was the most selfless thing anyone had ever done for her.

She knew her request was the height of selfishness. But it was all she could think of to get some semblance of her life back. She couldn't rely on Mark forever.

Despite what he'd said about taking care of her. They were from two different worlds. She had to get back to hers before it was too late and Quinn sank her claws into Beau.

"So, will you do it?" she said.

Mark slowed down as they approached the gates to a ranch. The Bellflower Ranch said the sign on the gate. But she knew it had been rechristened the Purple Heart Ranch by its inhabitants.

Honey had heard about this place for injured soldiers, but she'd never visited. They weren't on the charitable donations radar. It seemed the owner, one of the soldiers, was wealthy.

Sgt. Dylan Banks had never mixed in her high society circles. He would've been a sought after prize at last year's ball, but he'd married a local girl with no family. Honey had heard Sgt. Banks's wife had come from the foster care system.

"I just have to take you to this ball?" Mark asked as he pulled the truck up to a row of quaint cabins that looked like tiny, rustic pool houses.

The sun was setting, but people were about. An eclectic bunch walked toward a barn. Most were in paired couples. Men had their arms wrapped around women that they looked down upon as though the women were stars on Earth. Honey had never seen real men outside of a movie screen with such expressions on their faces. Were these a bunch of actors?

"And you'll have to pretend you adore me," Honey said as she gazed at the loving couples.

Mark turned to her. His gaze held her in place. Inside, her heart warmed as though a small flame had been given life.

"Yeah. I think I can do that." His gaze raked over her one last time, and then he turned away.

Honey felt bereft without him beside her. But he appeared in another second at her door.

Opening the door, Mark offered her his hand. She didn't know why she hesitated. Perhaps because she knew that once they began this farce, her life would take a new turn? Honey slipped her palm in his. Tingles ran down her spine as his strong hand clasped hers.

"Welcome to my humble abode," he said.

Honey looked over at the quaint little cabin. Up close, it was even smaller than a pool house. "It's … nice."

Mark chuckled. "You don't have to lie. It's probably smaller than your closet."

"I don't have a closet anymore."

His thumb rubbed circles below her knuckles. "I don't have much. But what's mine I'll happily share with you. I'd never turn family out."

"I'm not your family."

"No." He waggled his head, not committing to her denial or claiming the affirmative. "But you are my responsibility now. First thing's first. Let's get you fed. All I've had today were those finger foods, and I'm starved for a real meal."

CHAPTER ELEVEN

"You're dating Dumasse's daughter?" Mark wasn't sure what irked him more. Chase's incredulity at the thought that he could pull a girl like Honey? Or ... well, there was no or.

Chase was right. A guy like Mark could never pull a girl like Honey. Not without it being a trick.

"It's not real," Mark admitted. "Something happened after you left."

Mark filled Chase in on the good deed he tried to perform that had turned into a complete mess. Chase's eyes went wide, then wider, then they narrowed, and finally closed in utter disbelief.

"You're telling me she thinks she can make this right if you pretend to date?" Chase asked.

"If I pretend I adore her," Mark said.

He looked across the room to find Honey. She'd been surrounded by the wives of the ranch. The women all wore open, friendly smiles. But Mark wasn't fooled.

He knew the meddlesome matchmakers, who'd each been matched themselves, were pumping Honey for information about the status of her relationship with one of the few bachelors left on the ranch. Just as Mark and Chase looked to add numbers to the Army, the brides of the Purple Heart Ranch were always looking to add to their ranks on the ranch.

Honey smiled politely at the women. Her head turning right, left, and center as she addressed each woman as they fired question after question at her. Each woman watched her with genuine interest. But Honey's smile didn't reach her eyes.

Mark wanted her to like everyone here. He wanted Honey to experience what real family, friends, and fellowship was like. She wouldn't find any better folks than right there on the ranch.

He also wanted to go over and feed her. Honey had a paper plate balanced on her knees. On it, was a small salad with no dressing. But she hadn't taken more than one bite.

"This place," sighed Chase. "It got you, too."

"What? No." Mark shook his head violently. "I'm

helping her out. Her father disowned her. Who does that?"

"Henry Dumasse, that's who."

Dylan Banks, the man who had made the whole ranch possible for Wounded Warriors to come and heal walked up with his pregnant wife on his arm. The man wore shorts that showcased his prosthetic leg, a souvenir from his time in the armed forces.

"Dumasse's wife wanted a divorce," said Maggie Banks. "But he demanded sole custody of their two girls. He made the girls choose which parent they would go to live with. Honey chose her dad. Her sister, Ginger, chose her mom. It was all over the papers years ago."

Mark couldn't fathom his parents apart. Much less making their children choose between them. It seemed to him the height of child abuse.

"That's not the worst of it," said Banks. He turned back to Maggie to complete the story. Maggie had lived there all her life and would know all the town secrets.

"He left his ex-wife and daughter near penniless," said Maggie. "He wanted to make them pay for leaving him and making him look bad."

"What judge would allow that?" asked Mark, outrage building in his chest.

"They didn't go to court," said Maggie. "I think Carletta Dumasse knew that her husband had many officials in his pocket. He owns so much land and businesses here. Ginger went from private schools to public schools. She's a couple of years older than me, but I remember her. She and her mom were always in church. They went from wearing designer clothes to secondhand, but they always looked happy to me. I only saw Honey in the papers. She has the same eye color as her mom, but she never had that same sparkle as Carletta. Her mother passed away before Ginger went off to college."

"I've had a couple of run-ins with Henry Dumasse," said Banks. "He makes Ebenezer Scrooge look like Glinda the Good Witch. I can't understand why any child would choose to stay with such a man."

"I can," said Maggie. "I understand that need for comfort and normalcy having grown up in foster care. After a time, you stop looking for love and settle for security."

Maggie looked down at her protruding belly. Bank's arms tightened around his wife. Mark's gaze went to Honey.

Maggie was right. Her eyes didn't sparkle. But some of the tension in her shoulders had seeped out. Now she was leaning slightly forward in the huddle of women instead of back.

Reegan's and Beth's gaze lifted and turned to Mark. Their lips tilted conspiratorially. The two women didn't hide the fact that they were discussing him.

When Honey met Mark's gaze, her smile spread slightly. There was a spark of something in her gaze. But before he could be sure, she looked away, her cheeks reddening.

"Wow," sighed Banks. "What is it about this place?"

Mark didn't bother to answer that rhetorical question. This ranch, where love sprouted quickly and unexpectedly, had not gotten to him. But if he were honest, that woman may have.

Honey had his protective instincts firing on all cylinders. He felt the urgent need to show her a different side of people after the childhood trauma she had gone through. Mark took a deep breath, then made his way into the den of lionesses. The women fairly purred at his approach.

He held out his hand to Honey. "It's a nice night," he said. "Want to go outside?"

Honey's lips parted. She nodded and slid her hand into his. There went those tiny pinpricks of sparks again.

"Ooh," the other women singsonged like they were in grade school.

Mark tried to hide his annoyance at their adolescent ways. But, on the other hand, he and

Honey were pretending to be in love. They might as well get some rehearsal time in.

Before heading outside, Mark stopped by the spread on the table and filled up two plates with barbecued ribs, corncobs, and rolls.

"You have a healthy appetite," Honey said, eyeing the piles on the plates.

"These are for the both of us."

"I can't eat that. It's all sugar and carbs."

Mark scooped some green salad into the corner of one of the plates. He squirted some dressing on the top.

He led Honey back to his place. Instead of going inside, he indicated the plastic chairs on the deck. Honey smoothed her skirt and sat gingerly. Mark had a strong desire to muster up. But first, he wanted her fed.

He placed the food in her hands. She eyed the plate as though it were filled with worms.

"Not a fan of barbecue?" he asked.

"I've never had any."

"But you're from Montana."

"Eating ribs and corn on the cob were not covered in etiquette manners at finishing school."

"You're not in finishing school, or at brunch, or with that nose in the air society. Let your hair down and dig in, woman."

"Okay." She giggled, looking around. "Um ... where's the knife and fork?"

"Right here." Mark held up his fingers and wiggled them before digging into the food.

Honey looked down at her plate. Her fingers hovered over the glazed meat. She had a couple of false starts, hands getting close and pulling back at the last second. Until finally, she picked up one rib.

She nibbled tentatively at the saucy slice of meat. A slow smile spread across her face. She took another bite, this time just a touch less dainty.

"This is really good," she said. "You guys should sell the stuff."

Mark didn't bother to tell her the sauce was store-bought. He felt far too satisfied watching her eat and smile and relax.

The night birds serenaded them. A gentle breeze brought the sweet smell of flowers from the garden. The moon shone down as their own personal nightlight. If this had been an actual date, the setting would've been perfect.

Mark set his half-eaten rib back on his plate. His belly felt full and content even though he had only had a few bites. He tipped his head back with a grimace of defeat, glad Chase and Banks weren't around to witness his realization.

Wow, this place. It had finally gotten to him.

CHAPTER TWELVE

Honey slept deeply. It was the most peaceful rest since the last time she'd laid tucked in her mother's arms. Her mom had crawled into her or Ginger's beds a lot when they were kids. Honey never knew why she didn't prefer the city-sized bed she'd shared with her dad. Honey loved those nights when she got to sleep inside her mom's hug.

Sleep was the only time she allowed herself to think about her mother. In the waking hours, if her father caught her staring off into space, he'd accuse her of wishing for her mom. As a child, he threatened to send her to live in the one-bedroom apartment that her mom shared with her sister.

The one time Honey had visited her mother

there, she felt closed in by the small space. The walls were so thin, she could hear the neighbors. There was dust on the couch that had smudged her white dress.

Honey had panicked at the stain. Her father expected her to be perfect at all times. She would get in so much trouble for that.

Her mother had let out a weary sigh and then went to work scrubbing out the smudge. There had been sadness in her eyes when it came time for Honey to go. But for the short time Honey had been there with her mom and sister, they'd each looked happy, carefree. They walked around barefoot in faded shorts and T-shirts. Honey didn't own either garment in her closet.

Her mother's hair had been down, her face scrubbed clean of makeup. Honey remembered thinking how beautiful she looked. It was one of her last memories of her mom.

Honey had chosen her dad over her mom. To keep her dad's favor, she hadn't visited her mom often. And all too soon, her mother had gone to heaven.

Honey opened her eyes now. The first thing she recognized was that she wasn't in her own room. The space wasn't much bigger than her mom's apartment bedroom had been. This room was smaller than her en suite bathroom. The sheets were thin, the comforter scratchy. There was noise coming from the open window; laughter, conversation, animals. She was not at her father's home.

It all came back to her. The shoe. Her dress. Her father. Beau. Mark.

Then more.

The group of women who'd flocked around her in the barn last night, whispering secrets about Mark like they wanted her in on all the private jokes. Mark pulling her away to be alone with him. The sweet tang of over-cooked meat dripping in sauce.

Honey still had the salty-sweet taste on her tongue. Her fingers still carried the spicy scent. Sucking at her teeth, she came across a kernel of corn stuck there.

If her father could see her now, he'd disown her all over again.

She didn't care.

It probably had something to do with the fullness in her belly. She'd finished off her meal last night leaving nothing behind. She'd slopped up the sweet sauce with not only her dinner roll but Mark's buttery roll as well. That's probably why she'd slept so well. She'd likely gained five pounds.

She didn't care.

That and the fact that Mark hadn't been satisfied

until her plate was clean. No man had ever cared that she ate. Her father cared what she ate, only the finest and not too much so as to not put on any weight.

She put her bare feet on the floor. Her hair was down around her shoulders. She had on not a stitch of makeup. She felt ... happy.

She should be in a panic about her future. But the sun shone into the windows. Wafting along the breeze was something that smelled good.

Honey gathered clothes from her case. She knew the bathroom was across the hall, having used it last night. Padding barefoot on the tiled floor, she reached for the door handle. It turned and opened on its own.

Honey was met with the tanned wall of man-chested muscle. Mark stood in the bathroom door, wearing only a towel.

"There she is," he said with a grin.” You sleep well? Don't worry, I left enough hot water for you. You okay?"

No, she was not okay. She had no idea where to look. Not at his bare chest that glistened with water from the shower. Not down at the towel covering his private bits. Not at his bare feet with neatly clipped toenails. And definitely not up to his face in those dark roast eyes, dark enough to be reflective glass. She could just make out her reflection.

Her reflection. She wasn't wearing a lick of makeup, and her hair was a rat's nest. And she was in pajamas.

Honey covered her face with a yelp. "Don't look."

"What's wrong?"

"I'm a mess."

"Are you kidding?" He chuckled. "You're even more beautiful without all that makeup on your face. I know women don't believe guys when they say that, but it's the truth."

He slowly peeled her hands from her face. His smile was genuine as it had been every second she'd known him. Mark might like to joke, but he wasn't one for games.

"Hop in the shower and get dressed," he said. "Breakfast will be waiting for you when you get out."

Breakfast? Last night she'd eaten enough to keep her satisfied for days. But at the mention of food, her stomach grumbled.

Mark's dimples made a morning appearance. "I think that's your tummy telling me it wants some more real food; bacon, eggs, toast, hash browns with a side of fruit salad, of course."

All that food should not have sounded appetizing. But her belly grumbled again with what sounded like excitement. Mark chuckled, giving her arm a squeeze.

"Let's get dressed and get you fed," he said again. "I gotta get to work."

"Work?"

Was he leaving her? A sense of vulnerability washed over her. Honey had no idea what she would do today without him. She had no idea what her role would be there except as his pretend girlfriend.

"Yeah," he said. "I help with the JROTC program. Another soldier here started it, but he's off on his honeymoon now that his wife is on a break from college."

Mark's hand was still on her arm, squeezing gently. Honey's eyes dipped to his chest as he spoke. A droplet ran from his shoulder down his bicep. It was on a trajectory to slide down his fingers and land on her. But it evaporated before it finished the downward slope, as though it didn't want to leave his person. That totally made sense to Honey.

"Are you one of those girls who needs an hour to get ready?"

"I can be ready in twenty ..."

His gaze narrowed.

"Okay, thirty minutes." Especially if she went light on the makeup. "Don't leave me behind, okay?"

Mark's features sobered. "I would never."

The moment felt important. But also too large for either of them to manage. Especially since they weren't fully clothed. Or in a real relationship.

"I'll be out as quick as I can," Honey said.

She twisted from his hold and ducked inside the warm bathroom. Though she clutched her clothes to her chest, she felt somehow bared to her soul.

CHAPTER THIRTEEN

With the knowledge that Honey was watching his every move, Mark stood with his back straighter. His deep voice took on a bass note as he instructed his young troops. By some miracle, the kids did marginally better today.

Billy got his left and right foot straight. Mark was certain it had to do with the intact sole of the shoes on his feet. Janey even gave Billy a look of approval at his improved performance.

"Sir?"

Mark kept sneaking glances at Honey out of the side of his eye. She leaned against a white picket fence, watching him with a grin. He was too far away to tell if the grin was the polite, bland smile she often wore or something that was a bit more impressed. Before he could be sure, Honey turned away as Maggie waddled up with her pack of dogs.

"Sir?"

Mark turned back to his troops. They were at the end of the field, marching in place in front of a fence.

"Should we turn? Or about-face? Or just bust through the fence?" Eli Wilson asked.

"At ease," Mark said.

When he turned back, Honey was walking off with Maggie. She tossed him a wave over her shoulder. Mark raised his hand in response.

"Dismissed for the day, cadets."

Mark hadn't given that order. He turned to see Banks grinning at him. Chase walked behind the other sergeant, shaking his head at Mark as though his friend were a lost cause.

The kids peeled off, headed into the barn for their things. They gave each soldier a high five as they passed.

"Word on the street is that you're taking Honey to the Debutante Ball," said Banks. "Oh, man, I'm sorry for you. I was forced to live through those nightmares back in New York."

"I escaped them," said Chase. "Since they're always over the holidays, I always volunteered to plan the family vacations and made sure we were far away from society. Off on an island somewhere or on a ski resort."

"Smart man," said Banks.

Mark looked between the two men. Sometimes he forgot that Banks and Chase were from money. The two men looked and acted so, well, normal. Not at all like the stuck up men he'd met the other day at the brunch. And the two men would never leave a man or woman behind or kick them out of their unit the way Henry Dumasse had done his daughter.

"You'll need to get a top hat and tails," said Banks.

"Honey said I could wear my uniform to the ball," said Mark, nearly stopping in his tracks. His uniform was as fancy as he got. He was more a jeans and T-shirt kind of guy. He didn't even own a suit.

"Oh, there's more than the ball," said Chase.

"Yeah, there are rehearsals, and more brunches and luncheons."

"Luncheon? What's a luncheon?" said Mark

"And don't forget about all the networking and schmoozing that goes on," said Chase.

Mark groaned. He hated making small talk. It was all so fake.

"I had to take the daughter of a count to one of these things once," said Banks.

Now he had to learn how to bow? Honey didn't say anything about networking or royalty. He thought he'd simply escort her there, eat some snobby food, look at her with goo-goo eyes so others would get jealous and that would be it.

"You'll need a crash course in etiquette," said Banks.

"Etiquette?" Mark sounded out the big word slowly.

"Yeah," said Chase. "You know, which fork to use, which spoon."

"Wouldn't I use the one on the table next to my plate?" asked Mark.

Banks and Chase looked to one another. Their expressions were part pain as though their memories of their time in high society were painful. There was humor also etched in their expressions as though ready to live through and make fun of Mark vicariously.

"It would be easier if you just married her," said Banks. "Then her reputation would be restored, and she'd have someplace to live."

"Marry her?" Mark choked. He looked around, but Honey and Maggie were already stepping into Maggie's and Dylan's home.

"Yeah, I mean you've already seen what's up her skirts," said Chase.

"Hey!" Mark came to an abrupt stop. He glared at his superior, the man he respected above most others.

Chase held up his hands in mock surrender, but his humor wasn't gone.

Mark was surprised the man wasn't more upset. After all, Mark had lost them the perfect location for the recruitment center. But then again, Chase wasn't dependent on that income. The sergeant could afford to wait the time it would take the government to cut through enough red tape to set them up with a place on their own dime. Mark couldn't afford to wait that long. Which was why he had to make this work and soon.

But just the pretending to be in love part. He wasn't falling for Honey. He couldn't possibly take care of her. He liked providing for her with what little he had. He liked waking up with someone he looked forward to seeing. He liked that she'd seen him working. He did want to get married someday, but he had to be sure he could take care of his family. He certainly couldn't meet the needs of someone like Honey.

"There's food and then dancing," Banks was saying. "You do know how to waltz?"

Waltz?

Mark pinched the bridge of his nose. This was getting more and more complicated. Exactly what had he gotten himself into?

CHAPTER FOURTEEN

"Aunt Maggie, Carlos took the pooper scooper from me. I haven't had a chance to use it."

Honey blinked twice, trying to ensure she heard the kid right. They were both of Hispanic descent. Honey didn't speak a lick of Spanish. She'd understood every word the little girl had said though. The words just didn't make sense.

"There are five dogs," Maggie Banks said. "Trust me, you'll get a chance to scoop some poop. Now go back outside, you two."

Maggie's tone had been patient and kind. Had it been her father, Henry Dumasse would've turned red at such an interruption. His bellows would've shaken the plaster of the attic walls.

The little girl huffed and stormed out mouthing under her breath. Those words Honey didn't comprehend. They'd had a definite Spanish lilt.

Maggie turned back to Honey, belly first. Honey hadn't had the occasion to be around many pregnant women. In the circles she walked in, most women were either looking for husbands or preparing to bury them.

"Sorry about that," Maggie said, lowering her body into a plush armchair. "I'm sitting them while their older sister is on her honeymoon."

"Is that Sarai?"

"No, you met Sarai earlier. Their sister is Eva. She's married to Fran. You'll meet those two soon. They'll be back next week."

Honey wasn't sure she'd be here that long. Although, even if her plan worked, there was no telling when she might move in with Beau. Or how long it would take him to propose. And then there would be the wedding planning.

She turned back to the woman who had welcomed her into her home. Maggie rubbed a hand over her round belly. Her gaze was soft and open, much like Honey's mother's had been. Everyone who she'd met here had the same look in their eyes.

Honey had already met a number of women on the ranch and a handful of the soldiers. Last night at dinner, the residents of the ranch walked in and out of each other's yards and houses without being announced. No one locked doors. Children and dogs and livestock were everywhere.

Honey brushed her hands over the fine fabric of her sundress. Maggie's home was neat and tidy. She needn't worry about smudges.

Dog drool? That was a different story. A dog sniffed at the toe of her heels. Then it laid its wet nose on her knees.

"Down, girl," said Maggie. "Sorry, are you not a dog person?"

Honey liked dogs. They just usually were the size that fit in her purse.

"I remember I used to see you at church during Sunday school when I was a kid," said Maggie.

"Oh, I loved Sunday school."

Honey had loved dressing up and sitting with the other kids while Mrs. Patel read them stories. Then they'd color and eat cookies. Her father hadn't approved. Too much riff raff, he'd said. And so he'd made their mother stop taking them. To Sunday school and church altogether.

"I don't get to church as often as I'd like," Honey said. "I have so many obligations now ..."

"I'd love for you to come with me this Sunday. Or, if you prefer more Bible study, Beth and Reece go on Wednesdays."

"Oh, I ..."

Why was she hesitating? She wasn't under her father's thumb any longer. She could spend every day at church.

Honey picked up the tiny dog and put him on her lap. Its paws smudged her dress. Honey rubbed at his back.

"That would be lovely," Honey said. "Thank you."

Honey looked out the window to see the two children who had been arguing were now playing together. The pooper scooper was forgotten in the grass. She and Ginger used to play like that, only quieter. And inside. But that was so long ago.

"Hey, Maggie."

A beautiful blonde came in with a baby on her hip and a baby bump on her belly. "Hey, your Mark's girl."

"Oh, I'm not his girl," Honey began but stopped.

Both Maggie and the new girl raised an eyebrow. Even the baby looked at her.

"We know the story," said Maggie.

"It's a good one," said the blonde. "The best one we've had so far."

"Right? It's like something out of a historical romance novel," said Maggie.

"What are you talking about?" said Honey.

The blonde and Maggie looked at each other again. Then look back at her.

"You don't know?" said the blonde. "I'm Cassie, by the way, Xavier's wife. Every marriage here starts out ... as a means to an end."

A means to an end?

"Isn't that the definition of marriage?" said Honey.

"But here," said Maggie, "the means has a habit of turning into something true, in the end. Something deep, something long, and lasting."

"I give her two weeks, tops," said Cassie.

"To get married?" Honey sat up straight. The dog in her lap gave a yelp. "No, we're just pretending."

Cassie smirked. "We all were in the beginning."

"We could be wrong about you and Mark," said Maggie. "But we haven't been so far. Regardless, now that you're here, you're family."

"Can you take the baby for a second?" said Cassie, handing the baby to Honey. "His mom is on her way from work, and my back is killing me."

Honey made space for the chubby little boy on her lap beside the dog. "He's not yours?"

"I honestly can't keep track of who belongs to who," said Cassie as she plopped down on the sofa and kicked up her feet.

Honey had never put her feet up on a piece of furniture. But neither had she held a baby. Somehow, it all felt natural.

"See," said Maggie. "You're already one of us. Kids and dogs are the best judges of character."

The baby gazed up at her and let out a chortle of delight. The dog panted at her other side, dribbling onto her dress.

CHAPTER FIFTEEN

"The ball begins with a grand entrance of the debutantes. Each girl will walk in on the arm of her escort. In some balls, girls are assigned two escorts."

Mark raised his brows at that. "That's very liberal of them."

Honey sighed, looking tired and exasperated. Her eyelids pinched in. She crossed her arms over her chest.

Mark bit his lip to say no more. He didn't like the worry on her brow. He definitely didn't want to be the cause of any furrows there.

"An announcer will introduce us," she continued now that she had his full attention. "The audience will applaud politely."

"Like at a graduation ceremony? My family brought blow horns."

"Why?"

"To make a scene."

Honey's brows furrowed again. But he figured this time it was in incomprehension as to why anyone would shout at the rooftops at their kid's accomplishments. Wow, her family was not normal.

"I bet your school and your family followed the hold-your-applause-until-the-end rule?"

"Of course," she said, turning up her palms as though it was obvious.

"Of course."

They were in their dining area. It couldn't be called a dining room as it was an extension of the kitchen. Honey had set the table. But the table was overrun with dishes and silverware.

"After the grand entrance is the dinner," she continued.

Now, it was Mark's turn to sigh. Suddenly, he felt tired and exhausted. "You should know I'm more of a finger food kinda guy."

"Oh, excellent, there will be tons of bread served."

Mark hid his surprise that there would be carbs served around the debutantes. He decided not to make a joke of that. They had enough on their plate.

He frowned again, looking down at the mass of cutlery.

Honey walked around the table to one of the two seats. Mark hurried after her. He did know enough to pull out her seat for her. Once she sat, she snapped open a napkin and laid it across her lap.

"The napkin goes on the lap when you start eating," she said. "Then it goes on the table when we're finished."

Mark took his seat, snapped open his own napkin, and then looked down at the daunting task before him.

There were ten pieces of silverware on the table, and they were all on his place setting. Honey had her own set of ten. She reached for the tiny pitchfork looking utensil with only three prongs instead of the normal four. Mark followed suit.

"Oyster fork." Honey held up the pitchfork.

"Oysters?" Mark blanched.

He wasn't a picky eater. He was just baffled at the rich folks. All the money in the world, and they dragged the bottom of the ocean for food.

"Salad fork. Salad knife."

She pointed to two utensils smaller than the oyster fork. But there was another set that looked normal sized to him.

"We can't use these two?" Mark asked, picking up the regular looking utensils.

"No, you can't." Honey pressed her hand to her chest. "You eat dinner with dinner forks. Dessert with dessert forks. And so on. Utensils are tools. Each one has a purpose."

"Like guns? You wouldn't take a handgun into the desert, would you?"

Honey looked at him blankly. She gave her head a shake and served some of the leftover ribs from the other night. Instead of using her fingers, she picked up the normal sized knife and fork and began carving into the dish.

Mark sliced the meat, keeping his knife in his left hand. The foot was nearly in his mouth when he paused. Honey stared at him again.

"What's wrong now?" he asked.

"It's customary to put your knife down after cutting a bite and placing it in your mouth," she said.

"Every time?"

She nodded.

Mark set both utensils down, leaving the meat untouched. "Maybe I'll be on a diet that night," he said with a grin.

Honey put down both her fork and knife. The creases in her forehead didn't make another appearance. Instead, she worried her hands. "I'm sorry. I know this is a lot. But if it is going to work ..."

She picked up the salad fork and set it next to

the dessert knife. Mark took the large fork and put it back in its place. Then he took her hands in his.

"Hey, I'm here for you. I'm just joking. I'll stop. I'll take it seriously."

Her blue gaze looked washed out, like the sea after a storm. "You think it's ridiculous, don't you?"

"I think it's important to you," he said. "So, it's important to me."

And just like that, the calm waters in her eyes settled, and a ray of sunshine broke through. "Why? You don't know me."

"I know you're a good person."

"Am I? I'm so worried about impressing other people that I'm forcing you to be someone you're not. You all do more good on this ranch in a day than I have done my whole life. Working directly with the children instead of putting money toward a cause to support them. Working with each other and supporting one another in the smallest things. To me, that's big."

"You're helping me."

"Only after you helped me first."

"I'm not keeping score. Tell me what's next. What happens after dinner?"

"There's dancing, but you don't have to do that."

"In for a penny, in for a pound."

Mark rose and extended his hand. He held his breath and let it out in a gush when she placed her hand in his. The tiny sparkles had upgraded into bona fide fireworks.

In for a pound? If someone else from the ranch could see him now, they'd say he was in for a band of gold.

CHAPTER SIXTEEN

"**D**o you know how to waltz?" she asked as she put her hand in his.

"I know how to salsa," Mark said, pulling her into his embrace. Left arm at a right angle, right hand at her low back.

"Those are two very different dances," she said, trying for some semblance of decorum. She was finding keeping cool and bland to be an impossible task around this man.

Sparks. They raced through her any time he touched her. But he had a magnetic personality. Mark was either making her laugh or frown. There was no bland smile for him.

"How so? You lead a lady around the dance floor. How hard can that be?"

His fingers curled around her palm, and she felt

the heat. His palm burned into her back, but she didn't try to escape. She gave in, trapping herself to him. He'd held her before, during the most embarrassing moment of her life. Now, he was trying to help her through the most important moment of her life.

"Four steps in a circle?" he asked.

"Three. Three steps."

Honey began the counts. Mark was a quick study, and soon he took the lead. He smiled down at her, dimples blazing.

"Told you," he said. "I got it. Nothing to worry about."

For the first time in a long time, Honey wasn't worried about anything. Not whether there was a wrinkle in her outfit, or a hair out of place, or any emotion on her face. She relaxed in Mark's hold and let him sweep her away, just like when he carried her from prying eyes.

"I still can't thank you enough for everything you're doing for me," she said as they glided across the small space in his living room. "Everything you have done for me."

He shrugged those broad shoulders. "You'd do the same for me."

Would she? They didn't run in the same social circles. Would they have ever met if she hadn't gotten stuck in that pavement? She realized how perfect those shoes had truly been to hold her still in time enough for him to come to find her.

"I have a trust fund," she said. "It doesn't mature for another year when I'm twenty-one. But it's more than enough to build a recruitment center."

Mark halted mid-glide. Their bodies were bent slightly as he'd been about to turn her. Slowly, he straightened, but he didn't release his hold on her.

"I'm not taking your money."

"Technically, it's my father's money. You were going to do business with him before we met."

"That's is different."

"Because I'm a woman?"

"No. Because you're you."

The emphasis on his words made her heart flutter. But her brain needed clarification. "What does that mean?"

Mark took a deep breath, clearly searching for words. He let her go, and she felt bereft, unsteady on her feet. She wanted to sink down onto the cushions of the couch, but she held her ground.

"You said I was family," she said. She was embarrassed to hear a tremble in her voice. She was terrified that he hadn't meant what he'd said to her. What everyone on this ranch had insinuated; that she might belong.

"You are." His arms came back around her, but not in a dance partner's hold. This was a lover's embrace. Both arms wrapped around her torso. Both hands sealed at the small of her back.

"But still, my money isn't good enough?"

"No," he said. "Money is what you have, not who you are. I only want who you are." He shook himself as though he had said more than he meant to say. "So, yeah, if you just introduce me to people like you planned, that will work."

"We can work together," she suggested.

"I like that. I need you." He winced like those were more words that weren't meant for her ears. He cleared his throat and tried again. "Because I'm not good at schmoozing."

"Okay."

"Okay."

They were closer then prudent for a waltz or a salsa. They also weren't moving in counts of three. They were standing still. Still and close.

Honey tasted the sweet tang of barbecue on his breath. She could make out the fine lines on his lower lip that indicated he was thirsty. He looked beyond parched. He looked hungry.

She'd never been kissed before. She'd never danced salsa or the waltz in a man's small living room. So many new lessons. Now, she wanted a lesson from him in the art of kissing.

"Excuse me?"

They sprung apart. Honey knew people on the

ranch didn't knock, but this person wasn't from the ranch.

"Ginger? What are you doing here?"

Ginger stood just inside the screen door. It tapped her backside as it closed, and she took another step inside.

"Mrs. Patel called me and told me what happened," said Ginger. "I was on the other side of the state, but I drove back as soon as I heard. Are you okay?"

Honey tried to pull on the bland smile. But her lips quivered. Ginger took the necessary steps to be nearer to her and pulled Honey into a hug.

"He's a low and vile creature." Ginger's voice was almost a hiss. "Why didn't you call me? You know you could've stayed with me. You always have a place with me."

No. Honey didn't know that. After she'd chosen to stay with her father, Honey had assumed battle lines had been drawn. Only Ginger kept coming back to check on her. Just as their mom had always called to check in on her even if Honey declined to take the calls to stay in her father's good graces.

Ginger squeezed Honey's hand. Honey squeezed her sister right back. When Ginger's hold loosened, Honey had to fight her arms to unlock.

"You're the soldier who rescued my sister?" Ginger asked, turning her attention to Mark.

Mark offered his hand. "Private Mark Ortega."

"Only a Private?" Ginger took Mark's hand. "I'm sure Sugar Daddy loved that."

"Ginger," said Honey in a warning tone.

"Don't worry," said Ginger. "I didn't inherit the snobbery gene in my family. And it looks like you're helping to disabuse my sister of the trait. So, I approve."

CHAPTER SEVENTEEN

He liked the sister. Ginger would've fit in in the military with her no-nonsense attitude and quick wit. The sisters spent the night together in Honey's room. He heard them chatting late into the night. They slept in for breakfast and were now in the Great Hall for lunch. Couples outnumbered the two remaining single men. So, of course, the brides of the Purple Heart Ranch sat Mark next to Honey and Chase across from Ginger.

"You misunderstand me, Sergeant Chase," said Ginger. "I think a recruitment center is a great idea for the community. I just feel that a college education should be the first push for our young people."

"Not every kid is meant for college," said Chase. "That line of thinking short changes our youth.

They need to be told they are smart enough for post-secondary education.”

“You misunderstand me, Ms. Dumasse. It takes a great deal of intelligence to make it in the military.”

“I wasn’t attacking these young men’s intelligence—”

“Young men and young women, Ms. Dumasse. We also have programs for those past their prime years. Today’s militia is neither sexist or ageist.”

Ginger Dumasse narrowed her gaze at the man known as the Terminator. Both spoke with cool detachment. The passion for their causes could only be seen in the spark of their gazes.

“I went to college,” said Chase. “It was a waste of money that most of these kids don’t have. Being in the military is a life of service. It will give these kids a purpose and a paycheck.”

“So does a higher education,” Ginger insisted. “I serve, as well. I’m a warrior for this nation here on the home front. I just do it without a gun.”

“Problem with guns, Ms. Dumasse?”

“No, Sergeant Chase. I have perfect aim. I just know the pen is mightier than the rifle.”

“Should we separate them?” asked Honey.

“Not a chance,” said Maggie, who sat on the other side of Honey. “I hear wedding bells.”

"Sorry," Mark said into Honey’s ear. "You know how this place is."

He leaned into Honey and bumped her shoulder. He wanted to rest an arm at the back of her chair. Or better yet, around her shoulders.

But he was feeling self-conscious today. He'd almost kissed her last night. That hadn't been a part of their plan. But it was totally on his agenda now.

"Yeah," Honey said, her cheeks blazing. "I'm sorry. I know you're not that guy."

"Not what guy?" Mark leaned back so he could peer down into her face.

"You know," she said without any added clarification.

"No. I don't."

"Well, you're not the marrying type."

When had he said that? "Yes. Yes, I am."

"You are?"

"I want to get married."

"It's just, you said eventually."

"Yeah, eventually."

The silence in the hall caught Mark's attention. The debate between Chase and Ginger had gone mute. Many eyes were on them. Grins spread across smug faces.

"Someday," Mark said into the pregnant silence. "But not to get a ranch house. Even though I do love this place. I need to be in good financial standing before I take on a wife and family. It's the responsible thing to do."

Honey nodded, not meeting his gaze.

Those half dozen eyes around the table narrowed on him in disappointment. Wait? Was he missing something? Did she want a marriage of convenience? Well, that was a dumb question. She was angling for one with the debutante ball. Would she settle for him and the small cottage on this ranch?

But on what income? Even now, his extra pennies went to his family. He meant what he'd said about taking care of her so long as she was in need. He wouldn't leave her behind. His body was buzzing with the thought of providing for her.

No, actually that was his cell phone.

"Excuse me. It's my mom." Mark rose from his place beside Honey and went outside to take the call. "*Hola, Mami*. What's wrong?"

His mother was a no-nonsense kind of woman. She didn't believe in small talk. She was far too busy for that. Once a week she called to check on his health. But those were Sunday night calls. Today was Thursday. He knew if she was calling any other day, it was about money.

"We have an emergency," said his mother, confirming his assumption.

Mark pinched the bridge between his nose as he listened to his mother relay the injury her brother had sustained while helping out a neighbor. He wouldn't be able to work for at least a month, maybe two. That was crucial income his family would be missing.

"You said you were getting that new position with the recruitment center," said his mother. "Will you be able to give a little more this month?"

"Of course," Mark said. "I'll figure it out. Don't worry, I'll take care of it."

He didn't have the money. He had no idea where it would come from. But that never mattered before. Even if he picked up a part-time job, he would get it in time. What was he going to do?

CHAPTER EIGHTEEN

"Oh, Honey." Ginger breathed the words as she stepped into Honey's bedroom.

"You hate it." Honey looked at herself in the mirror. The dress that was meant to be her Cinderella transformation suddenly looked like she was smudged with soot.

Why did she let her sister help her? She knew Ginger hated all the society stuff. Honey remembered Ginger's come out ball. She'd been in a foul mood, but she looked beautiful in a dress that was much like Honey had had designed.

Their mother had already passed away by that time. Ginger was in her last year of college. She'd agreed to go to appease their father. But as Ginger stood in front of the mirror in her old bedroom, looking at herself in the mirror, she'd backed out.

Their father had nearly burst a blood vessel with how much he yelled about how his daughter's move affected him. It was always about him.

"You look beautiful." Ginger came and rested her hands on Honey's shoulders.

"You really think so?" said Honey. Her smile wobbled higher and wider until it killed her face.

"I wish Mom could see this."

Honey's smile faltered, shrinking in on itself. It began to fade into blandness.

"Oh, honey bunny, no. Don't go there. You don't have to shut down and put your show face on anytime her name is brought up."

"She's not here. She left."

Honey turned from the mirror. Because she no longer wanted to look at her face, which was so like her mother's? Or because she didn't want her sister to see the turmoil in her gaze? She wasn't sure which. Probably both.

"She didn't leave you, Honey. She ran from him. Our father is not a nice guy."

"Then why do you keep coming back?" Honey rounded on her sister, no longer caring about what she saw.

Ginger raised her shoulders in a helpless gesture. "He's still my dad. I keep hoping there's a kernel of good somewhere in him. But after this, after turning you out, I've lost all faith in him. Family doesn't do that."

Mark had said that to her. Now her sister, who'd never truly left, said it. But Honey had done that. She'd turned her back on her mother in fear of poverty.

"You were young, Honey," Ginger said as though she could read her mind. "We both were. We shouldn't have been forced to make that choice."

"I'm sorry, Ginger. You kept coming back for me. You and mom. But I was so intent on pleasing him. I understand why she ran now. I nearly buckled trying to live on his trophy pedestal. Luckily, my shoe got caught."

In the reflection of the mirror, Mrs. Patel's heart shaped necklace rested against her heart. The shoes that had brought her and Mark together were polished and again on her feet. They were her good luck charm. Honey giggled, tasting the salt of her own tears.

"You're going to mess up your makeup." Ginger sat Honey down at the small vanity. "I'll fix it."

Ginger set about doing just that. Honey closed her eyes and gave herself over to her sister's care. She had every confidence Ginger would make her pretty. But not as a trophy. As herself.

"So ... you and the soldier?" said Ginger. "He's

very *Officer and a Gentleman*. I heard he swept you off your feet at the Bachelors' Brunch. And now you're living with him."

"It's not like that."

"No? What's it like? I see the way he looks at you."

Honey's eyes slammed open, and she nearly caught an eyeball full of mascara. "How does he look at me?"

Ginger grinned. "The same way you look at him: with interest."

Honey closed her eyes, but she no longer bothered hiding. "He's handsome. He's kind. But he's not marriage material. He doesn't have a job or his own place."

"Isn't he opening a recruiting center? And this home is a pretty nice place. From what I understand about this ranch, it could all be yours with a simple I do."

Ginger said it with a smile. So, Honey knew she wasn't serious. Or at least she didn't think her sister was serious.

"I couldn't," said Honey. But her refusal was light-hearted. Was she actually considering a marriage of convenience to Mark?

She'd always known her life would come down to that? But she believed she'd marry a man in her social class. She'd always assumed she'd have a loveless arrangement. But every time she thought of Mark, her heart fluttered, her cheeks heated, her breath caught.

Mark had means of his own. It had only been a couple of days, but Honey felt warm and cozy in the little cabin. She could take care of it on her own, no need for servants. Or maybe two days a week for a cleaning service.

"I'm not saying you two need to get married. How about just dating?"

Dating Mark? Honey already knew she liked living with him, dancing with him, sharing meals with him. They'd almost kissed, and she knew for certain she would like that.

A knock sounded at the front door. Then it opened without their acknowledgment.

"Honey?" called Mark. "You decent?"

"It's him," said Honey.

Ginger brushed one last layer of color on Honey's cheeks. "You're ready."

They opened the door. Mark stood in his uniform, filling it out as no other man could. He grinned wide and then his mouth went slack when he saw her.

"I'm sorry," he said. "You just took my breath away."

Whatever color Ginger had put on Honey's

cheeks was likely getting washed out by the heat that resulted from that compliment.

Mark offered Honey his arm, and they headed out for what she'd always thought would be the most important night of her life. Only now she realized it had nothing to do with the ball.

CHAPTER NINETEEN

He was a walking cliché.

There were butterflies in his stomach. Birds flying around his head. His heart beat fast and hard like a gong pumping out of his chest. He was every cartoon character's technicolor manifestation of a man falling hard.

"Where's your truck?" asked Honey.

They walked down the porch steps towards a dark sedan. Since all the soldiers here drove some version of a Ford or Chevy with a flatbed in the back.

"We couldn't show up to the ball in that. Besides, I wouldn't want to get your dress dirty. This is a rental."

He'd taken his grandfather's watch off as well and left it on his bedside table. He wasn't taking any chances tonight. It had to be perfect for her.

"Can you afford this?" The moment the words were out of her mouth, she grimaced. "I mean, I don't want you to go through any trouble for me."

Money was tight, but he wouldn't skimp on this night. He would show her the night of her life if it bankrupted him. Which this one-day rental had come close to doing.

"Woman, you are nothing but trouble."

He opened the car's door for her. Her body brushed his, and that spark between them ignited into a full-blown fire. Honey gasped, looking up at him with those doe eyes.

Mark resisted the urge to pull her to him and taste her lips. Though he had the right to. They were pretending to be dating. If the occasion called for it tonight, he'd certainly be willing to play that part.

But what about tomorrow?

He'd have to leave this place soon. With his brother laid up and the recruitment center on hold, he had to go back home and lend a hand to his family. Even though he knew his duty, he didn't want to leave Honey behind.

But he couldn't take her with him. Not to his family's two-bedroom apartment that currently housed four people. Mark would be sleeping on the couch when he went home. Where would he put Honey? In his dad's recliner?

No. Honey deserved better. Not because she

came from wealth. Because she had a big heart. But the people in her world hadn't bothered to look past her designer labels to see it.

Mark did. So did her sister. So did the people on the ranch.

Maybe he could work out something with Banks where she could stay in Mark's cabin for the remaining time he had? Maybe she could go with her sister?

He wasn't sure what to do? Already, the pressure to help his family overwhelmed him. But the need to provide for her was right on the same level.

"You good?" she asked, parroting the expression the soldiers often used.

He smiled down at the beautiful creature who had been entrusted into his care. She wore a gown of the finest silk. Her jewels were likely worth every penny his family had ever earned in their lifetime —times two.

"Yeah, I'm good," he assured her. And it was true. "I'm great. I've got the easiest job in the world tonight; making you look good."

That's all he would focus on and not that he'd have to leave and go back home to help his family.

He would enjoy tonight with her. He would present her to the world. He would get her back into the graces of high society, the place she wanted to be. That way, at least he'd know she'd be financially taken care of.

He could never afford to care for a woman like Honey. His heart beat a stubborn rhythm of revolt. Mark ignored it and got behind the wheel.

Twenty minutes later, they pulled up to what could only be described as a castle. Mark handed Honey out of the car amidst a parade of limousines. He wrapped her hand in the crook of his arm, tossing the keys to the valet who looked suspect at his rental.

Entering the ballroom, Mark had another shock. It was even grander than he'd imagined. Silver and gold were everywhere. Ladies dressed in white moved like graceful dancers on a stage, though they were only walking around the room.

"Miss Honey Dumasse and Private Mark Oregon."

Mark shrugged off the mispronunciation of his name. This was about Honey and not him.

All eyes turned to gape as they came down the grand staircase. Mark clenched his elbow so tightly he felt Honey wriggle her fingers in his hold. People's gazes slid past him like he was invisible. He always would be invisible to these people. Their gazes focused on her, where they belonged.

"Oh, Honey. We were sure you wouldn't show."

A raven-haired beauty appeared at their side. On

second thought, Mark decided to detract the description of *beautiful* from her. There was something dark and cold in the woman's eyes.

"Hello, Quinn." Honey smiled. Not the bland smile from when he'd first met her. Not the open one she'd adopted only a couple days at the ranch either. Honey's gaze was on Mark as she beamed brightly. "Why wouldn't I? I have been waiting for this day my whole life."

"After, you know ..." Quinn slid her gaze to Mark.

"Have you met my escort? Private Ortega."

"Only a private?" Quinn, who was barely five feet tall, managed to look down her nose at Mark. "Are you advancing soon?"

"I'm retired," said Mark.

"Oh," sneered Quinn.

"Mark is going to serve the community by opening a recruitment center. Already he works with the youth, teaching them about opportunities in the military."

Mark didn't correct Honey. Not in front of her nemesis. They could discuss his departure after the night was over. Besides, he liked the pride in her voice.

"Have you met my escort, Lieutenant Bryant?" The toy soldier who'd stood by during Honey's fall from grace appeared at Quinn's side. "He outranks you, Private Ortega. Don't you have to salute?"

"No, he doesn't," said Lt. Bryant. The man offered Mark his hand. Then he turned to Honey. "I'm glad you're doing well, Ms. Dumasse. I inquired about you with your father. I'm glad to see you're in good health."

The man's glance slid over Honey before turning back to his date. It was clear to Mark that the lieutenant was interested in the woman on Mark's arm and not his own. His heart thudded to a stop when he realized Honey could still have that engagement.

"Thank you both for your concern," said Honey.

She gave Mark's arm a tug to lead them away. Mark stalled for a moment. Wasn't this what she wanted? This was her way back in.

Lt. Bryant's gaze was an open door back into her world. But instead, Honey clung to Mark's arm. Like a puppy on a string, Mark did her bidding.

"Honey, there you are."

They came to another halt. This time before the imposing figure of Henry Dumasse.

"Dad? What are you doing here?"

"I wouldn't miss my daughter's come out ball," he said. "I'll take it from here."

Dumasse gripped Honey's hand, peeling her fingers from the crook of Mark's elbow. Honey yanked her hand away from her father.

"Mark is my escort."

"Oh, yes, yes. Thank you for your service." Dumasse took out a crisp one-hundred dollar bill. "And thank you for your service."

Honey snatched the bill away and crumpled it in her hand. "You're being inappropriate and rude."

Her father frowned down at her, a pulsing vein appearing in his neck. "What's this? A couple of days living in squalor has done you some good. The humility will be a good look."

Honey's features iced over. Her jaw clenched so hard that Mark worried for her molars.

"I'll give you the location you want for your center and a sizable donation to get started," said Dumasse.

Mark was slow to drag his gaze from Honey. She was his first concern. It took him a moment to realize Dumasse was addressing him.

The center? A donation?

That would be the answer to all of Mark's prayers. He wouldn't have to leave. He could take care of his family. He could still see Honey.

"Why?" asked Honey, suspicion dripped from her tone.

"We don't need to discuss this in front of the help," said her father, indicating Mark.

"Oh, he's the help all right," said Honey. "He helped me when you turned your back on me."

"And now I'm helping him. Beau is interested in

you. He came to talk to me after your … mishap. His father is on board with an engagement. A union between our families would be the merger of a generation. All you need to do is be a good girl and accept Beau's hand and everyone gets what they want."

CHAPTER TWENTY

*H*oney couldn't believe it. Here her father was again, forcing her to make another choice that was bound to hurt others while it raised his prospects. Her entire life flashed before her eyes as she gaped at him. What once was black and white was now filled with color. The color she mostly saw was red.

She remembered back to the time when she was a little girl, and her father had called her and Ginger in the room to make their choice. He'd stood in a corner, smug grin confident on his face. Her mother hadn't been looking at Honey. She'd been looking down at her hands crossed in her lap. Her mother had known then. She'd known that Honey wouldn't choose her.

Even knowing it, her mother had never made

Honey feel bad for it. She had never stopped calling. She had never stopped visiting. She'd always held out hope that even if she wasn't Honey's choice, she could still get some time with her little girl.

But Honey hadn't been mature enough to make any choices. She'd had spent most of her life trying to make sure she was chosen. Chosen by her father. Chosen by the right friends. Chosen by the right man.

If she allowed her father to make this choice for her, if she allowed Beau to choose her without even asking, she would fail not only her mother again. Honey would fail herself.

Unfortunately, choices were never that simple. In this scenario that her father laid out, it wasn't a win-win for everyone involved. Like always, he'd tipped the scales to make sure he would come out ahead, looking the best.

Sure, her father would have a business deal solidified. He'd be able to brag that his daughter had made the social match of the season. Ha, maybe even the match of the decade.

Beau might think he was getting a trophy wife, but Honey had discovered that she was so much more than that. In just a matter of a few days on the ranch with Mark, she had seen that there were different sides to her, strengths she didn't know, abilities she wasn't aware of. She wanted to explore those.

Then there was Mark. That's where Honey got tripped up. If she agreed to her father's demands, Mark would have everything he needed for the life he wanted. He would get the location for the recruitment center he was so passionate about, along with start-up funds. And he'd get them now instead of a year later.

When Mark's needs entered the equation, it should've been a no brainer. It was a no brainer. The decision made sense. The problem was her heart.

Her heart wouldn't allow her to open her mouth and agree to her father's scheme. Everyone else would win, but she would lose. She would lose Mark.

Honey's heart beat faster as she looked up at Mark. There was clear outrage on his handsome face. He looked as though he wanted to punch her father in the nose. He needn't trouble himself. She was going to slap her dad; verbally, not physically.

But before she could say anything, Mark stepped up. He put himself between her and her father. Instead of raising his fist, he turned and spoke directly to her.

"You should do it," Mark said.

Honey gave her head a little shake. Surely, she couldn't have heard him right. The man who'd nearly kissed her the other day, the man who looked as though he'd wanted to kiss her earlier tonight, didn't just tell her to take a deal where she married a man she didn't love for money.

"This is what you wanted," Mark continued. "It's your way back into the place you belong."

The place she belonged? Here, in a room filled with dozens of people who didn't lift a finger during her time of need. Here with a father who cared more about his bottom line than his daughter's well-being. Here with a man who didn't know a single thing about her other than her last name.

"I told you I'd make sure you were taken care of," Mark was saying. "This is the only way that I can see that you will be cared for in the manner that you're accustomed to."

Honey's throat constricted. Her lungs burned as though a match was scrubbing them clean. At the same time, she felt like she was drowning. And then there was relief.

Cool, soft, spicy relief as Mark pulled her to him into a tight embrace. Honey felt his chest rise and fall. Their breaths came into synch as he held her. But this wasn't a comforting hold. It was a goodbye.

Mark took a deep breath, stealing her air. With his exhale, Honey felt all the fight go out of her. How could she fight for the two of them when they weren't even a couple?

His body went tense around hers. Perhaps he was changing his mind? As she pulled away, she saw that Mark's attention was no longer on her.

"I understand why you're doing this," Mark said to her father. "You want to be sure your daughter is taken care of. Any father would."

Mark got it wrong again. That's not what her father was doing. This wasn't about her. It was about him.

"You've raised a strong, resilient, kind-hearted daughter, Mr. Dumasse. Be proud of her. Do right by her. As any father would."

The vein in her father's neck worked. Honey took a step into Mark, certain that at any moment, her father would roar loud enough to shake the chandelier.

He didn't. They were out in public. He would never cause a scene around his peers.

Mark pressed a kiss to Honey's temple. He gazed down into her eyes with a smile that didn't reach his eyes or spread far enough to dig into his dimples. He opened his mouth. Then closed it. In the end, he pried her fingers from his and was gone.

"That's my girl," said her father when they stood alone in the crowded room.

His girl?

His girl?

She'd never been his girl. She'd only ever been a prize in his trophy case. Well, no more.

Honey rounded on him. "I won't do it. I won't be a pawn in your game anymore."

He stepped into her. The vein pulsing again, but his voice was quiet when he spoke. "Think about your words, little girl."

"I'm not a little girl. I'm a grown woman. And you can't treat people like this, especially not your family."

She hadn't known that before. She hadn't understood the rules of family having been raised by such a callous man. Back on the Purple Heart Ranch, she'd seen people taking care of those who weren't even their blood. They cooked, cleaned, babysat, and scooped poop for each other just because they cared.

"He's not of this world," said her father. "He could never take care of you the way you need to be cared for. Besides, he was only in it for the money. Why do you think he left so quickly?"

Honey opened her mouth. But then closed it. Much as Mark had done a moment ago. Her father had a point there. Not that she believed Mark had done it for the money. The kids he worked with, the kids he was trying to lead to a better way of life, they needed that recruitment center for their start.

Just as he'd promised to get her back to a life she

deserved, he'd made the same promise to them. Mark was doing what he thought was right because that's what you did when you cared about someone you looked at as family.

"Come back to your world, Honey."

The problem was, this world no longer was right for her. It never had been. She'd had to sit silently in it, smile blandly, and never get a speck on her.

Well, no more.

She turned to see that the dinner had begun. Her father held out his arm for them to go in. Honey gave the man her back and walked into the room unescorted.

When she sat at her place, she tossed her napkin to the side. Ignoring the cutlery on the table, she picked up the piece of steak with her fingers and took a bite. Brown sauce dripped down onto her pristine dress as she smiled brightly at the aghast faces.

CHAPTER TWENTY-ONE

Mark folded his uniform in crisp, straight lines. He tucked the arms of his shirt in, then brought the collar to meet the shirt tales. Before placing the garment in his bag, he brought the fabric up to his nose and inhaled.

It was still there. Honey's scent. He was catching it everywhere that morning. In the bathroom, on the sofa, in the kitchen. She'd been in his life for such a short time, and she'd made a huge impact.

Honey hadn't come to retrieve her things last night. She'd probably forgotten about them and already replaced them with what she had back at her father's house. Or, maybe she'd gotten new things.

He'd refrained from going into the room she'd

claimed to immerse himself in her fragrance. He wasn't that pathetic. He eyed the door. It was cracked open. At the last second, he turned back to the task at hand.

Mark shoved the last of his things in his duffel bag. There was plenty of room left in the belly of the bag. He hadn't had much to begin with.

He'd be on the night bus across the states in a short time. Headed back to his parents' two-bedroom apartment in a low-class neighborhood where he belonged.

He'd tried to make something more of his life with his stint in the military. But it hadn't worked out the way he'd wanted. Now, he had to return to the real world and be the man his family depended on.

Because that's what families did for each other. They made sure that everyone was taken care of. Sacrifices had to be made.

Although Mark's parents would've never asked him to sacrifice his happiness for their comfort. They wouldn't have to. Mark could never abide by seeing his family in dire straits. Not when he could do something about it.

They'd scrimped and saved so that he could go to the military. They'd made do with what he could provide on his government pay. And they'd been proud to do it.

As any family would, Mark's parents, his siblings, they all wanted to see him succeed. They wanted him to not only reach for but to grasp his dreams of being in the military. When he'd been medically discharged, they'd mourned the loss of that dream.

They'd been ready for him to come home and would've cared for him themselves if it hadn't been for the Purple Heart Ranch. This place had become a second home to him. The ranch and its inhabitants had given him a new life. But his time was up here.

There would come another time when he could give back to his country again. But for now, Mark was going home to contribute to his family's earnings.

He wouldn't take on the sole breadwinner role. They would all work together to lift each other up. That's what mattered at the end of the day. A man had to take care of his family.

He zipped up the bag. But the sound of the teeth closing his meager belongings in rattled him. He couldn't shake the feeling that he'd left something behind. But the room he'd lived in for the last two months was bare.

A knock sounded at the front door. He'd already said his goodbyes. The other three members of his unit had tried to pressure him to stay, even offering him the cash his family needed.

Just as he'd refused Honey's charity, he'd refused them. He worked for everything he earned.

Mark opened the door to find Banks standing on the other side. The man's prosthetic leg gleamed in the sunlight as he leaned against the door frame. His face was serious, like the sergeant he was.

"They said you were leaving?" said Banks.

"Yeah," said Mark. He hadn't wanted a send-off, and he'd knew that if word got out across the ranch, the wives would all insist on a big to do.

Banks shook his head. "But your job here is not done, soldier."

"Job? What job?"

"You took over the JROTC for Fran while he's been away."

Mark shrugged. "I was just helping out. Besides, that wasn't a job. It was a pleasure." Working with the kids had given him a new purpose while he'd awaited the fate of the recruitment center.

"Of course, you were helping out," said Banks. "That's what we do for each other. We're a unit; a family."

Mark bit at his top lip. In his mind, he was calculating days and bus schedules in his head. "I can stay a couple more days until Fran gets back."

It wouldn't make too much difference. He could spend his evenings calling around his hometown looking for work. Then he could hit the ground running as soon as he stepped off the bus a few days later.

His only hesitation was Honey. He didn't want to see her when she came to get her stuff; if she came to get her stuff. He definitely didn't want to hear any announcement of her marrying Lt. Bryant. That would gut him.

"I must not have told you that standing in for Fran came with pay," said Banks. "I assumed you knew."

Mark knew what the man was trying to do. He'd pulled this same trick earlier this week with Billy and the shoes. Just like the kid, Mark didn't want any handouts.

"I was talking with Fran this morning," Banks continued. "He said working with the JROTC and the Youth Program was too much. So, I'm looking for a permanent instructor for the JROTC program. I was hoping you might be interested. And when the recruitment center opens, you're free to do both and have a double salary."

Mark's mouth gaped open. He'd been set to protest this obvious ploy to keep him here and help out his family. The picture Banks painted was a pretty one, one he wanted to hang in his living room. But there was still one problem.

If he stayed there in town, he'd have to pay for

living space. He couldn't afford that and send money home to his family.

"Listen," Mark began. "I appreciate what you're trying to do here. But I can't make it work. I only have another month on the ranch before the zoning regulations kick in."

"Oh, that," Banks waved his hand in the air as though he were brushing the nuisance of a thought away like an annoying gnat. "That can be handled."

"It can? How?"

"You know how."

Mark sucked in a breath. But when he did, his heart kicked into gear. It pounded a rhythm he could no longer ignore.

"I can't," he said. "She's going to marry someone else. Someone who's ..."

Mark was about to say someone who was better for her, but the words wouldn't pass his throat. Was Beau better for Honey? Would the rich officer get a real smile out of her? Would he ever know the real Honey?

No. No, he wouldn't. Honey would be trapped behind her facade of fake smiles, fake family, and fake friends for the rest of her life if he didn't drop everything and go after her.

"I've gotta go and get her back," he said.

Mark dropped the duffle bag and rushed down the porch steps. It was time for him to go back and get what he'd almost left behind. Unfortunately, he didn't get far. His boot caught in a loose floor board of the steps. He tried to wiggle it free, but he was stuck.

"Can I give you a hand, sir?"

CHAPTER TWENTY-TWO

Honey stood off to the corner of the deck as she eyed her handiwork. She'd never held a hammer in her hand a day in her life. Luckily, Dylan had happened by and helped her with her plan to glass-slipper Mark. The sergeant had told her his plan while he'd helped her to enact hers. Mark had fallen for both. Literally.

"Honey? What are you doing here?"

Mark squinted as his torso turned to her, as though he couldn't believe she was actually there. Of course, she was there. This was exactly where she wanted to be. Exactly where she was meant to be. And now she had the man she wanted to start her life with right where she wanted him.

"I'm here for you. You didn't think I was going to let you get away that easy?"

Mark gave his foot a yank, but his leg wouldn't budge from its place on the floorboards. For a second, Honey worried he might actually hurt himself. She came toward him until she was standing on the step just above him.

"Like I said, this place gets to you." Dylan bounded down the steps and made himself scarce.

Mark slowly extricated his leg from the floorboards and came to stand on the level with Honey. "I was coming for you."

"I know." She rested her hands on his chest. She felt his heart beating through the fabric there. It matched the rhythm of her own heart. "But it was my turn to show up for you. That's what family does, right?"

Mark swallowed hard as he gazed down at her. His arms came around her in an unbreakable cage. "Yeah, that's what family does."

He bent down and captured her lips in a searing kiss, a claiming kiss. If she'd had any doubt before, she was certain now. Mark was her true end goal, and she'd just scored.

He brushed the loose hair from her face when he released her lips. "I was going to leave to go and help my family. But I don't have to anymore. I can stay here. I can be with you, which is what I truly wanted to do. Even if I had left, I would've come back for you. I could never have stayed away from you. Not with how I feel about you."

"I know," she said, resting her cheek in the palm of his hand. "I know how you feel because I feel the same way, too."

"You do? Because I'm pretty sure I've fallen in love with you."

"I love you, too."

Could a heart burst with joy? Honey was sure it could. Not only could she feel her heart pounding in her chest, but she could also feel the strong thump of Mark's heart from where her hand still lay on his chest. She'd never expected to have love in her life. Now that it was in her grasp, she didn't know how she could've ever lived without it.

"You said you'd take care of me," she said. "Now, I'm making the same promise to you."

"Honey, I'm not taking money from your trust fund."

She shushed him, placing a finger to his lips. He would be taking money from her trust fund in another year. Because if her new plan went right, they would be happily married by the time her trust fund matured. Then it would be their money, not hers. She'd wait to lay that on him until after the honeymoon.

Mark curled his fingers around hers, freeing his lips from her admonishment. "We're not taking your father's money either. No one here wants to be beholden to a man like that."

"You don't have to. I kept my end of the bargain."

She would've been here last night, but she had a bit of networking and fundraising to do. After the dinner, she paired up with Mrs. Patel. The two women had commitments from three donors and one organization to help house and fund the recruitment center.

Mark's brows shot into his hairline when she told him so. He pulled her closer, closing his eyes as though saying a prayer. It was Sunday. If they hurried, they might even make it to church service. Or better yet, they could listen in on Mrs. Patel's Sunday School class.

"This place," Mark said when he opened his eyes, staring around at the ranch. "Patel said that miracles happen here."

"He was right," said Honey. "You are my miracle. You are a work of divine intervention that was set in my path to make my life whole again."

"That, and there was not one but two Patels involved. Banks also warned me that those two have a direct line to the Big Guy."

Honey smiled at that. Mrs. Patel had always been a guiding light in her life, even when she couldn't see the woman. In fact, it was Mrs. Patel that had helped her choose the pair of shoes that had gotten

Honey caught in the cracks awaiting her own Prince Charming. She'd also been the one to send Ginger when Honey needed her most, putting her family back together. The woman was truly her Fairy Godmother.

"So, I suppose you're staying with your sister?" asked Mark.

"I am," she said. "But I was hoping to find a new place in a couple of weeks. I heard there might be a vacancy here on the ranch. At this address, in fact."

"There is a vacancy." Mark scratched at his chin. "It can be ready for you in two weeks. There is one catch, though."

"What's that?"

His eyes shown down on her with more love than she thought her heart was capable of holding. "I'll ask you about it later. Just know it involves jewelry and a white dress."

"Sounds like my kind of party."

EPILOGUE

Colin Chase watched the newlyweds as they twirled around on the dance floor. He was thrilled that Ortega, Cartwright, and Lucas had found not only the healing their bodies needed, but the loves of their lives on this ranch.

Banks had warned him that there was something about this ranch. That something would skip over Colin. He'd already moved into his own apartment last week, just after his last day on the ranch was up.

The magic hadn't happened for him, and that was fine. He didn't need magic. Reality worked well enough for him.

He glanced again at his crew whirling and shaking their bodies out on the dance floor. The party wasn't even close to dying down. Single women from the town swarmed the reception, on the hunt for any remaining single men. Chase backed into the dark barn to avoid capture. He was well trained in evasive maneuvers.

"Ouch."

Colin turned around, arms reaching out for the interloper of his quiet space. The small shaft of light revealed a brunette with crystal blue eyes that brightened the dark room.

"Ginger?"

Ginger Dumasse brushed out her Maid of Honor Dress in a huff. He'd seen her around the town bumping elbows with the lower dregs of society. But like him, she was from the upper crust. Getting her hands, or her clothes, dirty didn't come naturally.

"I'm sorry, Ms. Dumasse," he said formally, releasing her to her own reconnaissance. Ginger also didn't take kindly to anything that she viewed as patronizing.

"It's not your fault," she sighed magnanimously. "You didn't know I was in here hiding."

"What are you hiding from?"

"Not hiding, just resting." She leaned against the door frame and tilted her head back.

Colin could help notice the elegant curve of her neck. Or how her dress displayed her collarbones. He knew her shoulders were strong. He watched her in the last local debate with her opponent where she'd held her own, seeming far more prepared than the incumbent state senator.

"I just have to be *on* all the time," she continued. "Say the right thing. Smile just enough, but not too bright. Eat the right foods or risk getting photographed eating a hot dog or a kabob. And I love hot dogs and kabobs."

"What's wrong with hot dogs and kabobs?"

"They'd make me look like a caveman. Not a good look for any politician, especially a woman."

Colin tilted his head, still not understanding. But she was straightening and reaching for the door handle.

"I have no idea why I just told you all of that," she said. She plastered on the bright, political smile. Her voice took on that affected tone of overly-cheerfulness he'd heard in the debates. It's not how she sounded when she was on the ranch talking with her sister. "I love what I do and believe my platform is the strongest for the people of Montana."

"Ginger," Colin reached out. "You don't have to put on a show for me."

She eyed him. There wasn't suspicion in her gaze. There was a kernel of hope, as though she wanted to believe his words. Perhaps she wanted another person besides Honey that she could truly let her hair down with. Was he that person?

"It's not like you'll get my vote," he continued.

And just like that, her walls went up and her eyes shuttered. "Because we're on different sides of the aisle."

"No," he said with a grin. "Because I'm not a resident of the state. I can't vote."

"But you still don't agree with my platform or policies?"

Ginger had a sharp wit, clear intelligence, and a mind that probed issues deeply. He had enjoyed his few debates with her. But he didn't want to get into this with her. He preferred the times when they were in a group and talking about philosophical matters. Or better yet, debating the top five movies or songs of all time.

When he didn't answer her immediately, she conjured the answer she expected from him. Before he could open his mouth to stop her, she turned the knob.

Flashes of light greeted them on the other side. Colin's instincts from years in the Army kicked in. He pulled Ginger to him, shielding her with his body. It took his brain a few seconds to register that the flashes of light weren't dangerous. At least not to him.

"Congresswoman Dumasse, is this your new beau?"

"How long have you and the sergeant been dating?"

"What? Beau? Dating?

Colin looked down at Ginger. She looked up at him. Another flash of light went off and the twin gazes of horror at this predicament were immortalized in polaroid for all the state to see.

Although these two are on opposing sides,
they're about to be stuck in the same party of two!
You won't want to miss
In His Good Hands
the ninth book in the Brides of the Purple Heart Ranch!

Shanae Johnson was raised by Saturday Morning cartoons and After School Specials. She still doesn't understand why there isn't a life lesson that ties the issues of the day together just before bedtime. While she's still waiting for the meaning of it all, she writes stories to try and figure it all out. Her books are wholesome and sweet, but her are heroes are hot and heroines are full of sass!

And by the way, the E elongates the A. So it's pronounced Shan-aaaaaaaa. Perfect for a hero to call out across the moors, or up to a balcony, or to blare outside her window on a boombox. If you hear him calling her name, please send him her way!

You can sign up for Shanae's Reader Group at http://bit.ly/ShanaeJohnsonReaders

Also By Shanae Johnson

The Brides of Purple Heart

On His Bended Knee

Hand Over His Heart

Offering His Arm

His Permanent Scar

Having His Back

In Over His Head

Always On His Mind

Every Step He Takes

In His Good Hands

Light Up His Life

Strength to Stand

The Rangers of Purple Heart

The Rancher takes his Convenient Bride

The Rancher takes his Best Friend's Sister

The Rancher takes his Runaway Bride

The Rancher takes his Star Crossed Love

The Rancher takes his Love at First Sight

The Rancher takes his Last Chance at Love

The Rebel Royals series

The King and the Kindergarten Teacher

The Prince and the Pie Maker

The Duke and the DJ

The Marquis and the Magician's Assistant

The Princess and the Principal

www.ingramcontent.com/pod-product-compliance
Lightning Source LLC
Chambersburg PA
CBHW071806190726
48292CB00008B/2734